# WHAT KEEPS A STONE FROM FALLING APART

Also by Arn Lou


*Operation: Nibiru 2012*

# WHAT KEEPS A STONE FROM FALLING APART

**Arn Lou**

Bogkanten

**I**

"Pictures up! Quiet, please." The last chattering voices are quiet. Everyone's fully focused. All is silent.
The first assistant director shouts again:
"Roll sound!"
The sound mixer answers: "Speed!"
"Roll camera!"
The first assistant cameraman - the first AC - answers:
"Camera is rolling!"
An audible beep from the camera indicates that the film is rolling.
The clapper loader stands ready in front of the camera with the clapboard. He announces: "117, take one."
The clapper loader smacks the slate, brings it down again, and sprints away from the camera.
The first AC calls: "Set!"
For a moment the director sits motionless sensing the atmosphere in the room. Then he shouts: "Action!"


The window was ajar. Rain fell on the ledge.
Christian was on his way to shut it when his mobile rang.
"Yes, Christian speaking."
"... ..."
"Hello?"
"... ..."
"This is Christian Klerke. Who is this, please?"

"You have a kind voice."

"Who is this?"

"He hits me. He's going to kill me ... and Arnold."

"Who? I think you've got the wrong number. Perhaps you should try the police."

"I don't think so."

The line went dead.

"Hello?"

Christian turned off his phone and threw it away aggressively. The number was ex-directory.

It must have been a prank. Some stupid prank.

He tried to remember the woman's voice, but didn't recall having heard it before. Then he slammed the window shut.

He lay down on the sofa. He didn't like ex-directory numbers. They irritated him. It annoyed him to know that someone else could check who he was without him being able to do the same to them. He stared up at the ceiling. A smoke-coloured ceiling that had once been white. Scared now. Strangely scared. Scared by what she had said. 'He's going to kill me.'

Christian's gaze moved to take in the cheap furniture. It finished up fixed on the bright colours of the poster above the desk. The poster that made him feel calm. He didn't know why. He'd never even seen the object it depicted in real life. But he knew all about it: weight 900,000 tonnes – or there about. Around 2± kilometres long, and more than 25 meters wide. About 70 meters above sea level.

Two towers, about 150 meters tall, kept everything in place. An impressive feat of construction led by Joseph Baermann Strauss and built between 1933-1937 by nineteen members of the *Half-Way-to-Hell Club*. Nineteen people protected by the safety net suspended from one end to the other throughout the work on *The Golden Gate Bridge* – one of the most photographed bridges in the US. The bridge Christian so often admired from his sofa.

Christian tried to think positively. Tried to get started on another story, but was still shaken by the peculiar phone call. She sounded so truthful. So convincing. *Arghh, impossible*. Just some nutter, concluded Christian. He inhaled deeply and exhaled audibly. Then he sought refuge in one of his old stories and began to fantasize.

The theme was pretty much in place. At any rate the dramaturgy. Inspired by script writer gurus like Syd Field, and old hands Robert Towne, Paul Schrader and Shane Black. Yeah, even Paul Auster. And every time Christian lay, as he did now, on his bed, he was convinced that he'd finally found his style. His way of writing.

And no-one got to change his idea when he'd hit on something - no-one. Criticism and suggestions were seen as personal insults, an attack on his artistic integrity. What had Peter Hoeg written recently anyway? And what became of Ib Michael's Paramount manuscript based on '*Kilroy, Kilroy*?' Shane Black, he knew, had started directing rather than just writing.

Christian's attention turned to the content of the manuscript. The film's theme – and thought, once more, of all the times he'd caught himself in the act of starting over and beginning again.

Even his most recent text was full of edits and rewrites. In Christian's head things were supposed to be perfect the first time round.

The story could only live if everything was just right, right from the start. It could only be touching, true and original if it was told from the heart. Open and direct, without manipulation or interruption. A manipulative, artificial approach and you'd have a film that didn't ring true. Not artistically, he felt.

But a work couldn't flow like that when inspiration failed. Then there was just this need to produce something, something constructive. With thoughts to focus on and the next step of the plot and dialogue to formulate he could feel the resistance rising in him. A resistance so violent that he simply ground to a halt.

It was then he remembered the 'two-line' concept ... and that he'd promised himself never to use it.

It was a very simple idea. Write at least two lines a day – and keep these two lines until the story was finished. When it was finished, then and only then, were alterations and editing permitted.

But he couldn't stop himself. And every time it happened he ground to a halt. He always had to just take a quick peek. A need which, once again, ran counter to his intention of only writing when he was inspired.

Christian was confused. It was all very confusing. Despite this he remained optimistic – stubbornly optimistic. Yes, that was what he was. Stubborn as hell.

Christian laughed to himself. He wanted, he could, he dared, he had to. Succeed, win, beat and conquer.

His attention wandered from his conclusion to the woman he'd recently had.

What was it? What was it he'd said to her? Was he writing his dissertation or had he already finished it?

Of course it all depended on who he'd talked to, but he just couldn't remember what he'd said to her – not this one. It wasn't because he wanted to meet her again. It was just good to know. Just in case. And think, what if he'd actually said something wrong. The thought was almost unbearable. Embarrassing. Terribly embarrassing. Still, it had worked as he'd intended, and that was the most important thing, he thought. It couldn't have been all wrong.

He had attended university hadn't he? At any rate it seemed the natural thing to say. Now he remembered. The intrusive questions dismissed with vague accounts of a break from study and serious consideration as to the topic of his dissertation.

He'd used all his standard phrases, which meant he was *taking a break from his media studies course doing proactive research in the field*. The woman had been a student. That was it. It all came back to him now.

Then he'd sat for a moment. Just sat there giving her time to digest. Getting ready to fire off his trump card. Right up between her legs. Almost casually. Not over-hyped or passionately. No, the delivery was more relaxed, without being self-conscious. The sort of attitude that came across as meaningful and serious. Which automatically invoked respect and moist thighs, as he liked to think.

Christian had said that he was making a film. On the side, whilst finishing off his studies. That he was a director and had been a first AD on several features, and that he wrote manuscripts in his spare time. He had directed a couple of short films once upon a time hadn't he? Whatever else you could say, he lived the dream. You couldn't take that away from him. The dream he shared with thousands of others. The dream of a particular career. A career in film. Of being famous. Of being a film director.

Even though, at times, Christian almost seemed to prefer isolation, it wasn't that he lacked friends. He just had trouble relating to them. He was constantly nervous that he might do something wrong. Saying something stupid, for example. That would have been unforgivably embarrassing. But you'd never have known it. He was too good an actor. So good, in fact, that he often convinced himself. So good that he sometimes doubted his own feelings. His own self. And even though his friends might have thought the same, they'd forgotten about it long ago. Friends who dreamed his dream. Friends who thought like he did, and that he could talk to and share everything with. After a fashion.

When one of them asked after his family, for example, they'd almost always have to drag the answers out of him. After all what was there to say about his family background?

It wasn't that he didn't want to. He just couldn't. 'Where was it you grew up?' 'A suburb.' 'What about your family?' 'Yeah, a mum and a dad and a brother and a sister.' 'What do they do then?' 'Bit of this, bit of that.' He was scared, both of saying too much and of lying. On the other hand he also felt that he owed them some sort of answer. A comprehensive answer. Honest and truthful – and that was the difficult part. This was where his brother's life always came into it. How this had happened Christian couldn't really remember, but it was a good way of turning the direction of the conversation to something less hazardous. Away from him. To something he felt he could control a little better. After a while it had just become routine. More than that, in fact. It had actually become a sort of compulsion that took over him every time the subject was raised. Almost like a tic. It always began with a certain reluctance – and with very quick short sentences – words like, living in L.A. ... Hollywood ... And when, quite naturally, the follow up question came, the answer was that his brother was a filmmaker. Not someone you'd have heard of. But, yes, a director. There were lots of them after all. Even though Christian tried to keep a nonchalant tone it was always a topic that made people listen with a mixture of enthusiasm and jealousy. Your brother? A director? In Hollywood?! Cool! Wow! That's far out! And repeat ... each time Christian reluctantly told someone else, it was as if he grew a little, even though he never acknowledged it. Even though it had never been his intention. His day just always seemed to get that little bit better. Especially when there were women listening. It was more interesting telling women that sort of thing than men. Women made better conversation and were generally more interesting than men, that was Christian's opinion anyway.

Women. Christian's women came and went. Not very often though, in fact far too infrequently. That was the picture he'd built up anyway.

If he missed out on a date, felt sorry for himself and sat and thought it through, he often came back to the idea that it was probably because he wasn't very extrovert. Yes, there wasn't really any getting away from that. He was more the sort of type that grew on people when they got to know him better. Not the sort of relationship it was possible to build in a hectic big-city nightclub, as he concluded. Anyway, that sort of thing was beneath him ... Christian never went to nightclubs or discos. Not anymore anyway. If truth be told it wasn't something he'd ever done much. No, nightclubs were for the young, the really young; for celebrities and all the wannabes. Intellectual artistic types, people like himself, went to cafés. This notion was, for Christian, now all but irrevocable. He spent a lot of time in cafés. Especially the 'movie' café in the heart of the city centre where film folk hung out with all the models in a delicious confusion.

Here he sat then, daydreaming and considering. Sometimes he used to imagine himself in the café in the company of some really famous actor or other. A friend of his. Typically, this fantasy coincided with the rough periods. He'd be sitting there discussing things and exchanging views. Both about films and about life in general. Of course, his friend the actor was dying to play the lead in Christian's first film. Of that there could be no doubt. That was why they'd arranged to meet in the first place. And while they sat and talked about how they would secure the necessary funds, they always remembered to smile. To smile relaxed and casually to the women who defiled past, but remain completely unaffected by the buzz their mere presence was enough to generate. Next, a similarly famous producer would step through the door. He would, of course, greet the actor as a dear friend and would then be introduced by him to Christian.

Christian needed a mentor, as he said to himself. Someone he could trust. Someone who believed in him and his manuscripts. That would make everything so much easier. It was the way things were so often done. If he was going to have to go it alone, to apply for a grant from the talent development pool, for example, then sure, he'd do that. Christian was utterly convinced that it was only a matter of time before he'd succeed. Before he got the funds to make not just '*a*' film but '*the*' film. Especially this time, when he'd really put an extra effort into it. When he'd analysed the film consultant's professional background and thought he knew everything about their likes and dislikes.

"Cuut! Let's take that one more time, please. I thought it was a little too practised."

"All right, final checks, please." The makeup performs her last minute adjustments. "Quiet please." "Roll sound!"

"Speed."

"Roll camera!"

"Camera is rolling."

"117, take two."

"Slate, please."

*Smack!*
"Set!"
"Aaand ... action!"

**2**

Darkness. Light. Food. Darkness.

There was never really room for a baby. The flat was too small, and there was nowhere to get some peace and quiet. To get away from yet another one. The chest of drawers was moved. From the bedroom and out into the kitchen, where the mother always sat, when she wasn't at work or was just available.

Darkness. Light. Food. Nappy-changing. Darkness.

It was a small chest of drawers. Green with rusty hinges. Not very tall. About a meter, maybe a meter and a half. A cheap one. Bashed together out of recycled wood. But solidly put together. Not the sort of thing that fell apart.

One lay and clucked. Chatted and moved the little chubby limbs around in empty space. Already hunting for the blue hosteller. Bell rang – and a hand entered one's line of sight.

Back then, had one already understood the phrase 'God's punishment'? The hand forced the arms down against the side - darkness. Rattling from furniture. Shouts.

Crying from the drawer.

Noise and turmoil. A deafening and terrifying noise from above. Closer than normal. It had now reached the sides of the commode and its drawers. One cried louder and was now really terrified.

Then the feeling of sudden movement. Suddenly and violently back and forth.

Followed by the noise of puffing and scraping. The sound of a long series of blows. Until finally, after what seemed an age, the noise of a door slamming.

Crying from the kitchen.

# 3

One of the few things that really mattered to Christian was working out. Keeping trim. Fit for fight. Preferably three times a week starting Monday where he trained his chest and stomach and the underside of his upper arm. Next, on Wednesday, it was shoulders and back, stomach and legs, and on Friday it was time for chest and stomach again followed by the top of his upper arms.

To the initiated it was all a question of major and minor pectorals, triceps, deltoid, biceps, lattissimus dorsi, quadriceps and abdomen. And after a while Christian picked it up. It just became a natural part of his vocabulary.

Gradually the number of Weider- & Eleiko disks increased. Hand weights were raised and lowered. The handles of the training machine were extended and pushed, and the mirrors were used both for posing in and for catching sly glimpses of the others. Could muscles really be that big? – Impossible. Of course they were full of hormones, but anyway. No, there had to be a limit, thought Christian. There was no way he was going to get that big. It was just stupid. And it enlarged your heart and kidneys and gave you a bigger chin.

Even though Christian managed to convince himself almost every time he worked out of the ridiculousness of such proportions and dimensions, he still felt that something was missing. That the others had something he lacked, something undefinable. It was a constant source of irritation.

When he'd finished training he made sure he was alone in the showers and studied himself – always with a natural excuse at hand if someone should come crashing in. A comb, for example. So he could start innocently combing his hair. It wasn't good to come across as too self-obsessed.

Christian got up. The constant heavy bench presses and *flyings* and *pullovers* had extended his chest to a size 70A. It had taken several years of hard work. His stomach muscles rippled in just the right way under his taunt skin, nevertheless he worried that he had a tendency to both double chins and flab.

He straightened up. That helped with the worst of it. Kind of.

Bloody mirrors, he thought. You couldn't get away from them these days. Like magnets with opposing poles, simultaneously attractive and repellent.

Still, he went jogging too, so it couldn't be all that bad. Maybe it was his teeth? Were they yellowing? His hands were definitely too small. Sort of like a pianist's. Too thin. Too gay.

Christian clenched his fists. He was going to have to get something to train his hands with. One of those things with a spring you could clench and unclench again and again. He couldn't remember quite what they were called, but he knew what they looked like.

He packed up his stuff in his workout bag and cycled home.

Christian recognised the envelope as soon as he was inside the door. A big fat envelope like that could only mean one thing. A rejection from the institute. The Danish Film Institute in the centre of Copenhagen, anyway, they only seemed to employ dilettantes and swindlers. Pathetic amateurs who knew fuck all, and only supported projects developed by people with a track record in the industry. Anybody else might just as well give up. They were going to get turned down anyway. That much was obvious, said Christian to himself. He'd already been rejected twice – twice!

As he had so many times, Christian felt misunderstood, but he made no objections. Didn't call and complain. What was the point?

There was nothing to do but accept his fate. He crunched a couple of pieces of paper and slammed his coffee cup down on the table. He could feel a slight fluttering sensation and a pressure in his diaphragm. A couple of tears gathered in the corner of his eyes. He put a lid on it all and decided to forget it. Just forget it – onwards and upwards, as he said to himself.

He'd managed to get his foot in the industry door and found work quite often as a *video assistant* on commercials. Initially without payment, of course, but now it actually paid okay. Work that had just sort of happened without him having planned it.

He'd contacted a film producer in the hope of being hired in some capacity. Not that he had any clear idea of what he wanted to do – he hadn't dared to have plans at that point – he just wanted to be part of things.

The producer had mixed him up with the new production manager, however. And when Christian arrived there was coffee, pastries and a comfy sofa waiting for him. He'd had to acknowledge the mistake when the real production manager turned up shortly afterwards.

An awkward situation arose where nobody said anything. Christian was waiting for a response from the producer whilst the producer and the production manager were waiting for Christian to leave. When nothing happened, the production manager stepped in and asked Christian to leave his name and address, and said that they'd hire him as a runner. There wasn't money in the budget to pay him, but he could be a part of things. And there was free food, thought Christian.

In the film industry, people's theoretical knowledge didn't count for much. If there was anything they hated it was certificates and graduates. No, the best way was to work your way up, show enthusiasm and initiative and do anything that was asked of you – And the film school professionals? Well, they were just as talentless as anyone else, not that they wouldn't try to convince you of the opposite. That was something of which Christian was firmly convinced. And hadn't he always felt that way? At any rate, it wasn't a thought that had just struck him in connection with his rejection slip. The one he'd received after applying, mistakenly of course, to film school.

And what was it they actually wanted? Did they expect him to already be a director? To be able to show them a film he'd already made? *Fuck!*

Please attach forty-seven copies of twenty-five examples of your work preferably in DigiBeta format, where necessary as DVDs and blah blah blah blah blah. What the fuck were they on? What was the point of a film school if not to learn how to make films? What was the point if you'd already taught yourself how to do it? They weren't any good though. That was obvious from their pathetic, amateurish graduation films. As if mucking about in there for four years was a good idea. Why? What would it actually benefit anybody? There was no guarantee of a job when you finished.

And it was all financed from tax payers' money?! Just so a little clique of stuck up twats could run round experimenting at a cost of several million per pupil? So that they could *learn* to be artists. As if making films was art. It was a craft pure and simple. A craft which *sometimes*, sometimes could raise itself to another level, which was not the same thing at all. But oh no. They didn't talk about 'handiwork.' That was beneath them. Far, far too primitive my dear. No, no it was all inspiration, *Auteur*, avant-gardeeeee, *caméra stylo* and '*Ladri di biciclette.*' Christian was angry. In fact, all of a sudden he was furious. He always was when his thoughts began moving in this direction. When he thought about the film school and the way it was run. And meanwhile, without thinking about it, he'd chucked it - the envelope from the film institute - in the bin.

Anger was one of the few feelings where Christian felt himself on solid ground. There was no doubting anger. Other feelings were a bit more difficult. What was a feeling anyway? It was only temporary. Something fleeting – and therefore unreliable.

"Cut! That's still a bit too practised. It needs a bit more depth, a bit more understanding perhaps. Okay? One more time please."

The DP - the director of photography - and the gaffer - the chief electrician - confer briefly and agree to adjust the edge of the light from one of the floor lamps. The gaffer calls one of his assistants on the walkie talkie, gives him a couple of brief instructions and stands with a critical eye in front of the monitor. All the while the lighting technician, under direction, finds the exact position to correct the spill light using a 'flag,' a frame of thick black material placed on a metal stand.

"A fraction more. Stop! Put it right there. Do you want to have a look?"

The DP sits himself behind the camera and looks into the viewfinder. "That's it. Much better, We're ready."

"Ready to roll!"

Muttering and bumping.

"Quiet on the floor, please, thank-you. Sound!"

"Speed."

"Camera!"

"Rolling."

"117, take three."

"The boom's in the frame."

The boom operator lifts the boom further up out of the frame. "Okay." "Set!"

*Smack!*

"... and action!"


Christian sat on his own at a table at the back of the café. He'd exchanged glances with a woman at the bar several times. A woman who seemed happy and straight up and who chatted to everyone. But Christian still had difficulty getting it together to actually do anything.

Just then he saw another man who obviously had plans. Christian lifted his upper lip to reveal his teeth in a failed attempt at a sneer. To others it just looked as if he was smiling to himself. The man wandered over to the woman and started chatting. Smiling with lots of platitudes and a fixed gaze which, fortunately, didn't seem to be working this time round.

The woman laughed at the man's chat and rejected him in a friendly way and returned politely to her beer only when he had moved on.

The intermezzo had left a gap, a break, where everyone was occupied. A break that Christian saw as an opportunity – it was one he could fill. He got up and moved over to the woman.

On close inspection she seemed even more attractive than she had at a distance. He banished the thought that visiting bars was pathetic from his mind and instead concentrated on a quote from Ingmar Bergman that had been rattling around his subconscious for some time. *'Making films wasn't about seeing, it was about listening.'*

The woman was slightly older than him, about thirty. Slim, blond and considerably shorter than he was.

She talked a lot, a surprising amount in fact, as Christian followed the contours of her body under her green blouse. She was telling him all about her wild past which she'd spent with the lead singer of some world-famous band. How she'd inspired many of their hits. How the lead singer had channelled both love and lust into his lyrics. For *her* sake.

Even though Christian was attracted to her, he didn't try anything on. He just let her say her piece. When she finished he'd be waiting with the killer blow.

But, in that he was mistaken. As soon as she was finished with one story, she moved on directly to the next. The story of a world tour of Europe, Asia and the US. And Woow! Niiice! Okaay?! Wicked!

She was unstoppable.

Christian felt that he had to do something, and he asked if they should perhaps go back to her place.

But the woman just shook her head eagerly and laughed.

"No, no. Not now, not yet. Lets go and have a top up at the 24-hour bar."

This was all getting a bit too much for Christian. But it was almost dawn, he was still alone and still attracted to her. Lonely, not that he'd admit it. Calm. Unusually calm. No fear. Just delightful anticipation.

So Christian went along with it. Along to yet another stupid bar. This time with a pool table and burly drunks in all sizes and ages.

For a moment Christian feared he'd made a mistake. That the woman was in fact a covert pool queen who played badly at the start but ended up fleecing unsuspecting men and winning all their money. A sort of sheman, he thought desperately. Christian was comforted by the thought that she seemed only to be here for further drinks. And to talk, to go where words led.

He couldn't keep the thought from coming. And it irritated him each time. There could be no doubt now of her masculine side he had to admit that. Especially the way she held a bottle. And her totally unashamed burping. But she was still clearly a woman. Attractive. Christian struggled with himself. Something in him had started to rebel.

He glanced quickly at his watch. It was eight o'clock.

It had been morning for some time, and the rush hour was getting into gear. He took another look at her and could see that, fortunately, it was now time for the main course. The dish that Christian had now been looking forward to for some time. The dish that the woman now, finally, seemed ready to serve.

The pitch of her voice had fallen, the looks she was sending him were more inviting. She was getting a bit unsteady on her pins, but was still capable of delivering a passionate French kiss. Christian still didn't really know what it was he was after. Looked at critically, she was actually sleepy and less than charming. Nevertheless he was aroused. He was hopeful.

The taxi took them way out into the suburbs to a block of flats and a tiny little two bed apartment. Very different to what you'd imagine given the wild life she said she'd led.

It took a little while longer for Christian to realise that everything wasn't quite as he had expected it. Even though the living room was a shade of pale green. And not just the walls. The cushions were green as were the ornaments and cuddly toys she seemed to collect. And this despite the fact that the kitchen was sky blue and the bathroom was orange.

He checked the medicine cupboard. Opening it very cautiously whilst flushing the toilet to drown out any noise he might make. An old *Clear Difference* from

Estée Lauder, plasters, paracetamol, a thermometer, a couple of cotton buds and a small pile of cotton pads. Cloroquine in a box and a yellowy green tube of 5% aciclovir.

Christian turned on the tap and shut the cupboard. A pack of *Always Ultra normal* fell on his head.

He entered the bedroom.

The woman was lying naked in the bed, moving sensuously under a mosquito net. Only at that point did he realise that he couldn't go through with this.

Everything was pink, and Christian more or less panicked. Suddenly feared the worst. Feared for his life. Was overcome by an overwhelming feeling that she was completely out of control – could do anything. Even as she panted invitingly.

He was scared now. Just scared. He didn't know why. Perhaps she had a knife hidden under her pillow and was just waiting to stab him. He gave a really lame excuse. Said it was too late, and that he had to get to work.

He said goodbye quickly and hurried out of the door. Out into the refreshing morning air where he tried to control his breathing and dried his sweaty palms on his trouser leg.

All of a sudden he felt desire rise up in him again – could see that it'd all just been nerves. Considered turning back even though he knew that it was now far too late. She wasn't up to much anyway. And those colours – and that décor. She must be a psychopath, he thought as he tried to catch a bus. Then again … he should just have fucked her. She'd been naked, ready and willing and everything. It wasn't that he didn't know what he *should* have done. It was just that the colours and the mosquito net had done for him. On the other hand, he hadn't just come to admire the bloody interior had he? … And that crap excuse, about having to go to work after having been out on the town all night?! That was such an obvious lie. Next time he'd have to think of something better.

Christian recovered a sense of purpose and jumped on to the bus. Tired and exhausted, glad to be on the way home.

Christian tried to sleep. Suddenly irritated at the interruption to his daily routine. He could write off the next couple of days, he thought. He tossed and turned. Opened the window and rolled down the blinds. Closed the window again. Was sweaty and freezing cold. Was both hungry and thirsty without really being either. Considered his actions and cursed himself for having just done a runner. Felt suddenly motivated. That was what he was, he thought, and stood up again. Ready to write his way out of his defeat. He *could* have had a conquest. He *could* have taken her. And the episode would be a great addition to his next manuscript.

The manuscripts that had already been through the

mill at the film institute, just sat gathering dust. At least they had done up to now. After all, as someone or other once said: '*If at first you don't succeed. Try, try and try again.*'

Christian sat up and started work. Sat in his favourite chair and got his favourite pad of paper out. A pad that was just that little bit bigger than A5. Only when he'd written it all in the pad was it time to transfer everything on to the computer.

Christian wrote the first ten pages without stopping. But was then overcome by doubt. Was the bar story worth writing at all. Of course, it needed to be part of a larger story. But Christian didn't have that yet. If the main character was to meet a woman in a bar, then doing so would have to move the plot on, develop the story in some way. Maybe the woman should try to kill the main character? But why? Because she was scared of men. And why was that? Because she was a psychopath. And where did that leave the main character? Argghh, it was going to have to wait.

Christian suddenly felt like working out. Like doing something else. Something that wasn't this. Working out and staying fit was important. It was important to keep trim and not just languish and wither he thought to himself. Christian put his clothes on again, packed his bag, cycled quickly over to the fitness centre and began lifting and pulling and cursing and swearing. Surprised at his own anger, but blamed it on the lowest common denominator pop music that was playing on the gym's noisy stereo system.

When he'd finished training, he went to work. So that was out of the way too. He worked as a cleaner. Staircases, three different places in the same area. A job that meant that he could just about survive during the periods when there was no advertising work to be had, and which, at the same time, was so flexible that he could fit whatever else he wanted to do around it. The only thing he had to do was to make sure the stairs were cleaned once a week.

He woke up. Terrified and overcome by an unconquerable fear of dying. Suddenly remembered an episode from his childhood only to force it away again. Not now! But it was already too late. It had already served it's purpose. Removed his focus from the really pressing problem. The fear which, by now, he was stuck with, and his thoughts which were out of control. It sneaked around, changed shape and crept back in. And then it jumped him in a cowardly, scheming ambush. He had to do something, to get help. He called and was answered.

At dawn Christian found peace and slept for a couple of hours. After a series of long conversations with the spirit world. The world from which miracles could arise. The world that could prevent anything. Alleviate anything. Even death.

"Thank-you! Better, yes, that was better. But ... I'm not sure how to say this ... it's more as if it lacks substance, maybe. Yeah, a bit more nerve. A bit softer if you will. It's still a bit too uniform. Perhaps it needs to be a bit more varied. One more time."

"Final checks, please."

Final adjustments are made.

"Okay. Pictures up! Quiet, please. Sound!"

"Speed"

"Camera!"

"... rolling."

"117, take four."

*Smack!*

"Set!"

"... And, action!"


Christian fought with himself and his own patience. Fought to find a thread in his story without being able to find a clear answer. What he really wanted to do was to sit and think through the turning points. The film's key scenes where events took a sudden turn. A turn which was almost always a new challenge. But an unexpected challenge.

In actual fact a film script was quite a simple thing. It was all about getting the character from point A to point B and ensuring that he constantly encountered new challenges. Preferably so many challenges that it seemed as though he would never make it. That was what a film script actually was, thought Christian satisfied.

Then his mood swung, he became angry and began cursing himself. If he was ever to have any hope whatsoever of getting just one of his scripts accepted he ought to start taking things a little more seriously. Denmark was one of the best countries in the entire world for film-makers. Except perhaps Canada or France. And for that reason, because the conditions were so good, he couldn't just base his stories on vague and poorly formulated ideas. Quite the opposite. It was one's responsibility to come up with a thoroughly thought-out idea. A complete story. And that meant it wasn't good enough to just rely on the standard film clichés to move the plot along. He needed to do more. Much more. To leave the commonplace trailing. To be truly original. That was the only way to break through the media noise. He had to be able to tell his story in one line. A punchline.

That meant it was crucial to find the core of the story and write and rewrite the manuscript over and over again. Just having an idea was like having an arsehole. Everyone has an arsehole, thought Christian.

But when the story had fallen into place, then he could start to sort out the dramaturgy, the plot points and forms of speech and the point-of-no-return, the dialogue and the way the plot advanced - all that stuff.

Suddenly he hated himself and the pathetic way he went about things. He got up from the table and went over to the fridge to find himself a beer.

Once he was back in the living room he curled up on the sofa and lit a cigarette. He sipped his beer and began to analyse his recent nightmare. Only now did he allow himself to recall the events he had been so scared of. He knew that one thought led to another. But right now it didn't matter. Right now he was ready. Right now there was nothing that could touch him.

# 4

The windows were black. And behind them was everything. The evil and the terrifying. Everything that didn't bear thinking about – but which it was impossible to ignore. Behind them could be almost anything. God's punishment.

The thought that was most appealing was toys. The best toys in the world.

Then call Mum. Listening and waiting, hearing them in the living room. Call again. Hear the short sharp shouts of command, but remain happy. Happy not to be forgotten. Happy to be heard, but still frightened. Of the black windows and everything behind them.

Call again. Now also scared of the adults. But what was worst? God's punishment or Dad and Mum's anger? The noise of scraping and tramping. A door slammed. Then the sound and smell of Mum.

The mother that stood there in a pair of white knickers and a dirty bra. She said it was time to sleep in that lovely rusty voice. Answered that she mustn't be angry, mustn't be upset.

Reached out for her hand but it had moved.

She *was* upset. Why couldn't he just sleep? Why was he always such a burden? God's punishment. There were the words again. Being told it was time to sleep. In a voice that was cracking, close to tears. She was meant for better things. She definitely didn't deserve this. She just said it. To no-one in particular. The knowledge that she would soon get up and go back to where she came from. To the light and the warmth and the adult voices. To big brother and big sister who'd both been allowed to stay up late and watch TV.

Lying alone again. And the windows were black. A strange sound from the window. Impossible, at first, to determine what it was. Couldn't really see at all. Though something had happened – some change. As if something white had been attached to the window. And then everything suddenly became much clearer. In time with a rhythmic beating on the window.

It was a face. A face flattened against the glass with open mouth and wide open eyes. And a hand tapping.

Screaming and screaming and screaming from inside oneself. Screaming so loud that the sound of the door slamming was inaudible.

Running out of bed to the door. The door that was locked. Hearing an unknown man's deep voice: "That's the punishment for not sleeping."

Had one been more calm, it might have been recognisable. But it wasn't. Screaming still, and sobbed and wailed. Someone in the flat above banged the floor and struck the water pipes. Prayed to God not to be punished any more. Didn't really understand what the offence had been, but promised to do better. Whatever that was.

Never got an answer.

Was still scared, and now also guilty of a crime.

But there came a day when things got better. Where, suddenly, there was quiet and there was space. Where the mother was happier and had money for ice creams. It all just got forgotten and hidden away. Got told that God and the magic had been with them anyway. And was grateful.

They shared a secret now. Something the mother's family weren't to know. They lived in Jutland, a peninsula far from Copenhagen, and were seldom seen. But when they met everything had to be perfect. Mum and Dad had decided to leave each other. And that was that and no more. The other thing – which it was now difficult to remember – that was a secret soon forgotten. Soon forgotten.

Got charming tight-fitting shoes. Was corrected with arms held in place by the brother's heavy knees. Spat at in the mouth when trying to call for help. Was, however, always helped in fights with the big boys. Not that one was allowed to hang around the big brother, but could always get help and protection if it was needed. At any rate during the first couple of years of school.

That made for confidence. Confidence from the first day of school. Full of so healthy and well-developed a sense of enthusiasm, that the tables were for dancing round and the other children were for singing to. Spoke English and did sums. Played up and mucked around. Was the person at school that they all talked about. Even the bigger children.

Strongest when others were weakest. And, for several of the teachers, the exception that proved the rule. The child greeted with respect, an ally, greeted with secret signs and knowing looks. A hero. Without wanting to be one. Suddenly grown larger than all the others and stronger than most. Yes, there was more to come. Much more.

And things went on. Wounds became scars and only hurt when you laughed – at any rate that's what it said in the comics. Went to school and did homework, the mother found herself as a new and emancipated woman and the big sister had already left home long ago. With plans and a new and unfamiliar fervour in her eyes.

Threw stones at the *Stone collector*, a peculiar girl who went around on her own. And got the just as peculiar Thor to drop his trousers when he was staying the weekend so he could show off his enormous erection. Played hide and seek and marbles one year and changed to frisbees and yo-yos the next. Played football. Played *Luke Skywalker* and *Darth Vader*. Listened to *Wham* and *Duran Duran, U2* and *Michael Jackson*.

Got money for the forbidden cigarettes by nicking bottles. Got regular meals, had dental work done and did the household chores. Groped and French kissed Marie in the school bogs and was laughed at by the others when discovered. Had everything under control. Had dreams and made plans, like his brother, who, it seemed, had plans to travel and see the world.

Wanted to write. And wrote. Wanted to draw. And drew. And saw. Heard that the brother had left. Across the seas to exotic places and other countries. Over the seas to parties and beautiful women. Away from here. Dreamed of leaving too. Away from the suffocating care and the depleting islands of children. Away from the newsagent and the butchers, still there, a relic, on the corner of the street. Away from a life where time was quietness, and reserves were something banks had. Where ambitions and other impossibilities were for the braggart bourgeois and gossip column celebrities.

Away from the place where the evening light came from the television. And where it was enough. Enough just to be yourself. Where everyone *looked after* themselves. Where pretty children were abused and women got cheeks. Red wine cheeks. In the prim and proper suburbs with a few heretical and shameful blocks of flats dotted here and there. Like a blemish on the area's reputation. Where the quiet and resourceful Weissdorf in the flat upstairs was laughed at because he tolerated his unfaithful wife, and where the Turkish weirdo in the next stairwell drank petrol one day set it alight and killed himself.

Went to school through it all, dreaming by day, nightmares at night. Something else was needed, even though it gave some respite. In the empty flat the nights were the worst.

Avoided bed and wandered the house instead scared of its demons. The mother was busy with other things.

And if it hadn't been for him things would have been much easier as she said. The only thing to do was to pray things got better.

Walked around abandoned streets and gloomy cul-de-sacs. Pressed against walls or behind hedges when a car passed. The sweeping white light in the dark. If one was hit one would be dead by the morning.

Had so much anxiety that it hurt. And only when dawn broke and the day revealed itself was it possible to creep back to bed and get, at least, a couple of hours' sleep. A rhythm that, of course, wrecked the day, and his schooling and any contact with the normal children. A rhythm that, of course, resulted in a stream of complaints from the school's headmaster.

Would actually have managed anyway. If it wasn't for the fact that his voice had broken one day during one of the mother's seldom visits to the flat and had taken him to the doctor. A consultation which the only thing one could really remember anything of, was that one was sent out into the waiting room whilst the mother and the doctor discussed matters behind the locked door.

She was good at putting her case. And as far as the doctor was concerned it wasn't absolutely necessary that the patient himself was present.

A waiting room where one was too occupied trying to suppress the nausea caused by the clinical doctor smell to have time to be scared.

And when the mother finally came out it wasn't to

take him home. Even though that was what she had promised. First they had to stop off at a hospital and talk to a specialist. Someone who knew more about one's problem. And *then* they were going home.

And once again one was left outside to wait. In the white corridor of the children's ward with it's stupid drawings.

The mother came out from an office accompanied by what seemed to be a nurse. Because she was good at putting her case. And when one finally understood what the look in her eyes meant, it was already too late.

Two nurses had taken hold of one's arms and their grip tightened. Felt that they held one in with a vice-like grip. So she could go. Without a word. Without ceremony. Without turning round.

Cried. Screamed and begged for mercy. Promised to always be good. Promised never to do anything bad again.

They dragged one into a grey cold bathroom and took off one's clothes. Threw one down into a bath and scrubbed the skin red. Irritated and impressed by one's stubborn terror and committed resistance. *'Hey, come on. It's not that bad. Didn't you ever have a bath at home?'*

An iron grip on his neck was enough to let the other one get to him. But even though they tried sympathetic and kind words nothing helped.

In the end they put the kind words to one side. By the end they just sneered, called one a beast and beat the air out of one with a well-placed elbow in the solar plexus.

That was the way they did things. When they were fed up with irritating children that would neither listen nor look. That just screamed out of control.

The other nurse seemed to want to say something to the colleague, but it never came out. Just a question as to whether blows were necessary. The answer was many years of nursing experience. She ought to look and learn rather than ask questions.

When they took one to the operating table, even more hands were needed, one got almost superhuman strength from fighting for one's life.

The mask over the face which, one thought, would suck the life out of one.

The staff on the point of giving up, and trying loudly to explain what was about to happen, whilst they talked amongst themselves of demons and possession and the devil. A little kid with such unbreakable strength. *'And where the fuck are the parents?!'* It just wasn't possible. Not without influence from above or below. And then it worked. Quickly, in fact. The anaesthesia took effect and finally one gave up.

Christian was well into his second bottle of wine. Seriously considered contacting a psychologist. A bit like when he was seeing Sarah. But perhaps that was just something he imagined? And hadn't he managed very well without one? And what if they fundamentally changed his personality. Wouldn't that affect his creativity?

Christian turned up the music. The CD had reached Rodolfo's aria *'Che gelida manina'* from Puccini's opera *La Bohème*. He mimed along as well as he could - *Chi son? Sono un poeta. Che cosa faccio? Scrivo. E come vivo? Vivo!* – 'Who am I? I am a poet. What am I doing here? I'm writing. And how do I live? I live!'

Christian raised a toast to the air and emptied his glass, before the aria continued. Then he poured out a new glass.

# 5

Work on the latest manuscript was actually going well, first of all because Christian thought he'd found his story. All in all, he actually felt the manuscript was good enough for him to send it out.

This time it was a low-budget film with a spectacular plot about death, love and money. One that was always in fashion, and that would probably sit well with the producers' eternal quest to make money. That was the only thing they thought about, thought Christian. They might as well be selling sausages or porn. Just as long as the cash register rung. But there was no getting round them if you actually wanted to get something onto the screen.

This time he was going to bypass the Film Institute – no talent development funds – and go directly to the producers.

Even though Christian had had days or weeks where he hadn't been able to get anywhere, it had been a success in the end. And even though he had to fight against the desire to just give up, he'd pulled it together and kept on plugging away. Because he *must* succeed. He *would* succeed. They just had to give him a chance. God just had to give him a chance.

Christian called the first production company in the Film Institute Directory, and finally, after a number of unsuccessful calls got to speak to the producer.

Christian was nervous and fumbling. His coughing was

getting out of hand. That little cough, which always seem to take over at the most inconvenient times. Like now, for example.

Despite this, Christian managed to agree a meeting and was generally speaking fairly pleased with his efforts. Once he'd got going he actually been very well spoken and had talked for a long time.

The producer had been mostly passive, just asking a couple of initial questions, but had managed to sound interested. Pretty interested, actually, now Christian came to think about it.

So Christian was happy. He coughed even more – like a baying audience – and jumped around the living room in his excitement. Now was the time! Now there was a way through. Now it would happen. Now it would finally happen! *Thanks be to God. Thank-you dear, dear God. For being with me anyway.*


When they met at the producer's office later that week, it turned out that the producer hadn't had time to read the script anyway. They got sent lots of them, every week, he said, and it was difficult to keep up.

Christian was not discouraged, however. It was going to to take more than that. Much more than that. He improvised a pitch and said everything there was to say. The producer had to understand that this idea was simply too good. That this script had to be made into a film.

And the producer listened once more both positively

and patiently. Almost as he had on the phone. It sounded like a really good idea, but there was no money for development right now. It sounded like a *really* good idea though.

Christian tried to say that the script didn't need any development. That it was ready. Completely ready to be made into a film.

Either the producer wasn't listening or he chose to ignore what Christian had to say. He did promise to read the script though and they agreed to talk next week.

A week which came and went without any response, and which made Christian more and more uncomfortable. Something must have happened. Had he had an accident?

Christian called again. Asked if everything was okay. And was told that it was, but that the producer was away.

Then he was on holiday, and since then he'd been busy with other meetings. Meetings which actually took up the next two to three weeks.

After a day's hesitation Christian took contact to the next company. One that was considerably larger and could afford to employ both developers and script editors.

And the script was read and commented on. And it wasn't bad, though the plot was a bit slow here and there. The characterisation was also too weak and one-dimensional, and in many places the dialogue was just banal. What was most important, however, was the lack of structure. It was as if he had tons of ideas, but that they went off in too many directions. But he was welcome to call them for further in-depth comments and of course more than welcome to send them a rewrite. Without payment. Times were hard and they had a number of other projects in development, so the money, well that would have to come later.

That was where the world broke in. The growing hope that he'd finally succeeded, finally got through to someone evaporated and his confidence was flushed out with the morning urine. Nevertheless he forced himself to think the situation through and concluded, with a certain relief, that it wasn't worth listening to a bunch of amateurs anyway. Fuck them. It would be better to start a new script. Or rewrite one of the old ones.

Christian felt inspired. That was what he'd do. Re-write one. Of course, why hadn't he thought of that before?!

He took up the first script. It was a story about a beautiful woman who'd started a relationship with a guy she met by chance at a beach. The plan was for him to help her kill her rich husband so they could live it up on his money. But when that obstacle had been removed from their path, the woman chose to do a runner – leaving the male lead with broken dreams and a murder team on his heels. A really good story, when

Christian considered it, even though it did remind him of some film he'd seen a long time ago. But what did that matter? The important thing was the perspective. The unique angle.

And his discipline was back, and the days flew past. From one page of his pad to the next. With the entirety of his new story ready in his head. From thought to hand to pen.

And the evenings passed just as quickly. With the TV in the background all about a nineteen-year-old guy from Germany who'd killed sixteen people, for example.

And with psychology books during the evenings when he wasn't at the café, mostly spent sitting grumbling in a corner by himself. Confirming his own fantastic talent and the other's mediocrity.

But when the spirit took him he could suddenly, and when he least expected it, transform into a real charmer and the guy everyone had a laugh with. Overcome by euphoria. It was also, as a rule, when he was in these moods that he was best at scoring, at least that was how it seemed when he considered things.

But the course of love did not run true, he never really knew what it was he wanted, and he was always disappointed. In 25 years he'd only ever had one girlfriend with whom he'd actually been able to see some sort of future. And she'd left him.

Actually she'd always just been a bitch, he thought. Now when he could no longer remember her face. Only that her name was Sarah, and that her son was called Lucas.


"And thank-you!"
The usual murmur is absent. Everyone just stands around.
"Okay, let's take a break."
The first AD nods and turns to the team.
"Okay, five minutes everybody!"
Everyone apart from the director and the actors leave the set. On his way out the lighting technician turns off a couple of the hottest lamps.
Quiet.
"I think we should try running through the scene from the top. There's still way too much uncertainty in the way it comes across ..."


Two days studio shooting – a standard five thousand Kroner job. Christian hummed to himself and was satisfied with his set. A set consisting of a reference monitor on a medium-sized folding table, a further monitor on a C-stand – a versatile flag stand – plus a video tape recorder and a couple of video tapes next to the reference monitor. All strategically and routinely erected in a corner of the set. Now he was finished, there was time for a cup of coffee and a smoke.
He often smoked too much. Especially when he was stressed. He ought to be more careful, thought

Christian to himself.

Christian took a sip of the crappy coffee and smoked. He could have offered to help the others, but he preferred just watching them and making sure that his own house was in order.

A rail was positioned on top of the big rectangular wooden running boards that provided a more even surface than the pockmarked floor. When finished, the entire construction consisted of a couple of straight rails and one curved one.

It was only a minor shot, a short dolly track, but a complex one and that meant it could take some time getting the camera to move as intended. And then, of course, there was the model's acting ability, or lack of same, to contend with.

The dolly grip pushed the *Fisher* dolly into place with the help of one of the lighting assistants. The seat, the expander and the other bits and pieces were finally rigged and the beast was recharged again. The *Fisher* dolly evidently had problems holding a charge.

The key scenic artist and his assistants screwed and hammered a peculiar set into shape, whilst the property master wandered around adjusting the products that had been set up.

The first assistant cameraman provided assistance in rigging the camera, and a couple of ten kilowatt lamps – so called *ten k's* – were hoisted up on a couple of '*Gorilla*' stands.

A further distribution box was needed. The one they'd

hired made the fuses blow, and a runner had to shoot across town after another one, not just now, but now. The customer sat and chatted with the boys from the ad agency, whilst the director stood and told the photographer that it was neither him nor the agency who'd come up with the idea of using the stupid chair – it was the customer's wife. An Italian designer chair that just *had* to be used.

They laughed together secretively and conspiratorially as they agreed that it was ever thus.

But they were happy enough because they were fucking the ad agency, the agency was fucking the client and the client was fucking the wife.

Christian became angry. Without knowing why.

The people who'd actually devised the thing, the real creators, copywriters and ADs – Art Directors – yeah, they fucked themselves and never really got the hang of it all, thought Christian.

He listened at a distance. Discretely and anonymously. Sure they were celebrated from time to time, but people always associated adverts with the director who'd filmed them. When they were good anyway. When they weren't, it was always someone else's fault, he concluded.

This despite the fact that being a director was mostly just changing a picture here or there or making minor alterations to a storyboard. Deciding on a *Dutch shot* instead of a tilted one. Doing a camera move with a dolly instead of a Steadicam. Or, when the agency had just hopped on that particular bandwagon, using a director who could actually deliver plausible dialogue. As if actors couldn't think for themselves.

And for doing that a good director could pull down 150,000 Kroner a day.

Christian would happily have accepted half that and done the job at least as well and probably better. And the audience wouldn't care. They couldn't see the difference.

150.000 Kroner a day?! You'd only have to work ten days a year. Christian laughed to himself at the thought of how ridiculously the world worked.

Production costs for a commercial, depending of course on the scale and type of the work involved, were about 750,000 on average. On top of that came the ad agency's cut – which was a similar amount – preferably a little more. He just knew it. They were talking so loudly that everyone could hear it.

So there was a good reason for the director to laugh, a good reason for the agency to laugh, a good reason for the customer to laugh, he got sex with the wife, and a particularly good reason for the wife to laugh. The film was hers after all. Power to the adverts.

Christian was far away in his own thoughts and he swilled the scolding coffee down his throat without noticing that it burnt his mouth. Power to the whore company. Past greatness, where film directors were part of well-integrated artistic movements, entities that forswore prostitution, was forgotten. Forgotten too where the times when working in advertising attracted derision and curses. Just as forgotten as celluloid would be one day. The holy film celluloid that Martin Scorcese and other like-minded film directors would never give up.

But the first thing one forgets is memory. And money has no smell. And who else is going to pay the rent?


"Are we ready for the shot?"

"Perhaps we should try closing the set ... It's not because you can't do it, I know that. You're really good. But you have to let go. Have to put your heart into it, otherwise, I'm afraid it's just not plausible. I know it's difficult all this. But we're going to have to do things this way. If we don't make this convincing then we're not telling the story. And we lose sight of what we're trying to do. We want to be heard."

The First AD stands waiting at the edge of the set watching the scenery. He looks at his watch and knows that he's going to have to break in in a minute if they're to stay on schedule and get the day's work done. He begins instinctively to consider other solutions, when the director turns around and nods understandingly. The AD turns on his heel and hurries out ...

"Sound!"

"Speed."

"Camera!"

"Camera's rolling!"

"117, take six!"
*Smack!*
"Set!"
"Aaand action!"


Christian's little flat had a kitchen, a bedroom, a living room and a toilet. It was on a main street. Just behind some old film studios on the next street – in fact, he could see them if he stood up on a chair in the kitchen. And he sometimes did.

The flat had no shower, just a minimalist toilet you had to back into. A flat Christian had obtained from a slightly dodgy estate agent.

They happened to get talking after a session in the gym, after the guy had overheard Christian talking on his mobile phone about needing a place to live. The house in which Christian rented a room was for sale now that the 79-year-old owner had died of a heart attack in his garden chair.

The preening and bustling wife had knocked on Christian's door one morning and, almost whispering, told him she wanted to speak to him. Suddenly so slow moving, her movements delayed. Suddenly so old looking.

Christian had expected something to happen now her husband was dead, but had been surprised at how quickly it all happened. After discussing things with her children, the wife had decided to sell the house and buy a little flat where she could live more comfortably. She couldn't manage the garden any more. Definitely not on her own.

Christian had actually liked his room. He'd been far more happy with it than the first one he'd had, with the overweight daughter, Ulla, who was probably still living at home even though she was over forty.

The estate agent was one of those quick-talking over-familiar types who was ready to do any sort of deal at any time, preferably right now. He suggested to Christian that they go over and look at the flat straight away – and, if he liked it, he could have it. The rent was a bit steep, but not more than he could pay.

Actually, the guy had been okay. He'd even agreed to reduce the deposit by one month's rent. Christian couldn't therefore get angry when, later, he talked to his neighbour and found out that he actually paid twice the rent that everyone else in the block did.

The living room was nondescript. Full of the sort of furniture you'd expect to find purchased from a number of discount stores with a sofa and table, a TV and video and a cheap armchair. Knee-high shelving ran along one of the walls and it was stuffed with books.

At first they'd been meticulously arranged in alphabetical order, but in the last couple of years he'd taken sometimes to just putting them any old where and letting them all get mixed up together. The thought pleased Christian. Because, as someone once said, external order means internal chaos. But he couldn't quite resist the temptation. Not for more than a week. Then the books would return to their alphabetical order. But at least he'd proved that he could if he wanted to.

The bedroom was furnished with a cupboard, a chair and a cheap double bed with a headboard and bed posts made of wrought iron.

All the walls were white and plastered with film posters.

Even the toilet, where, admittedly the pictures were only postcard size.

Everywhere except above the desk in the living room, where the Golden Gate poster hung. Christian's favourite. A picture he could disappear into. A picture he could dream his way into. And the dream was always the same. Driving across the Golden Gate bridge in a red Ford Mustang convertible. With loud music and the warm wind in his face. On his way to Los Angeles. To the film awards.

No plants. That was too difficult. Too womanish. They needed constant care. He'd rather have a little plastic bouquet on the table. If at all. That'd keep forever.

Christian had got home too late to be bothered with cooking and all that and just bought a pizza. He sat and ate it whilst drinking his beer and re-seeing the German documentary '*Olympia*,' made by German director/photographer Leni Riefenstahl.

And he'd seen most of them. Right from *'Der Triumph des Willens'* and *'Unserer Wehrmacht'* to *'Jud Süss,'* directed by Veit Harlan.

His fascination with II World War Germany and it's leaders remained a great source of pleasure to him.

Christian philosophised over the pleasure involved in having all that power. Think if it were possible to visualise power so completely that it actually had a direct effect on one's own life. He got up from his armchair and lay down on his bed to meditate. Something that put him at his ease when he was tense, and made him feel energetic when he was drained. But Christian couldn't get started. He was constantly interrupted and disturbed by thoughts about his own life. Whether he'd ever succeed.

He got up again, went back to the living room and put a CD on. The soundtrack from *'Batman'* directed by Tim Burton.

He dug out Danny Elfman's pompous title sequence which he put on repeat. At which Christian walked straight into *The Kodak Theatre,* into the Academy Awards. The Oscars. That was how it always started.

As a nominee he had, of course, attended the obligatory lunch beforehand and chatted with all the others. With Steven Spielberg, James Cameron and George Lucas, for example.

His name had been called and he'd received his certificate of participation. He'd been informed of the appropriate length for an acceptance speech – not too long – and been shown where to go, how to get away from the podium after the award and out to the back of the theatre where the world's press were waiting for him.

A member of staff in evening wear would take Christian's place in the theatre as soon as he had been called up, as under no circumstances was the impression to be given that there were empty seats.

As the soundtrack built up to a crescendo Christian heard the famous actor who was one of the hosts for the evening say: 'And the Oscar goes to ... Christian Klerke – *Two-liners.*'

Finally Christian was satiated. He stopped the music, and was on the point of vomiting. He grabbed another beer and poured half of it down his throat straight away. He felt like he had after his hospital visit, where he'd been allowed to wallow unfettered in hot chocolate and cake. He remembered how, the day before his discharge he'd been more scared than ever.

White light. Creaking beds. Noise from the other children coughing, whimpering or just turning in their sleep.

They said that they'd removed his tonsils and that soon his voice would again be boyish and easy. That initially he could only eat liquids or bananas.

White light. Rattling trolleys.

Time to go home. Frightened anyway. Had whispered with one of the other boys, confidentially, about the bleeding.

The boy grassed. About the blood on the pillow.

A white pillow, turned so as to hide the spot. Blood, that suggested that the wound in his throat had opened. Blood that could mean he'd have to stay there longer. In the white light with the creaking beds and the rattling trolleys.

Still lying there. Silent, anticipating the judgemental words, with eyes fixed on the scratches in the linoleum.

Prayed to one's God. Had noticed the glazing bars. They formed a cross. A sign that couldn't be ignored.

One heard someone or other ask whether one was in pain.

The second time one shook one's head. No, it didn't hurt any more. One wasn't even sore, at least that was what one said.

They nodded smiling and let one go.

And the shadow by the bed was forgotten. And the blood and the boy.

But not God and his unforgettable magic.


During the first days the mother was home all the time. She broke the rules and let one eat cake and swim in soft drinks. She covered one in blessings and praise and ensured that one started up in school again. Said that things would now get better. Said that her new boyfriend had helped her so much.

One never really understood where this sudden care

came from, and it didn't last long. After the first weekend the mother felt that one was healthy enough to manage on one's own. One could always go down to the newsagents where she worked or phone. But only if it was absolutely necessary. The mother had a life too, and one didn't want to upset her, did one? Now it was time to be a big boy and thank one's God and the magic, thank them that one was healthy and back at home.

For the first time the demons began to visit him during the day. The demons which, otherwise were kind enough only to visit him during the night. One knew one had lost when one felt their presence like a hand on ones throat. A gentle pressure on the larynx. Just for a brief moment. But enough to let one know that they were there. They never said anything, but the sound was theirs. Every creak from the floor, every little noise from the stairs or the bathroom confirmed their presence. Their silent evil. The evil that, in the end, would drive one mad. And when one was mad, they had one in their grip forever. And then ... one knew no more. Couldn't manage anything any more. Just knew that one must avoid madness at all costs. Anything but madness.

One learned how to defend oneself. Not that it always worked, but it gave one a certain peace and comfort. Speaking to one's God and trying to understand his mysterious ways. It seemed to scare them. One listened. Not a noise. Found a method. Cough three times in a row. Like a spell. Like calling the Father, the Son and the Holy Spirit. And the demons were scared. That was what a girl at school had said. A girl who knew everything about God and Satan. A girl who came to school one day with her arm in a sling. She said that God had saved her from something much worse. What it was she couldn't say. Her father had asked her not to. It was one of those things one didn't talk about.

One called the cat. The kitten the mother had given one so that one wasn't alone now the big brother and the big sister were gone, and the mother spent so much time with her boyfriend.

The kitten was sweet. One wanted to pet it and stroke it. But it didn't like being looked at. Didn't like having its throat looked into. Nor did it much like one probing its genital opening. The kitten wanted to get away. It writhed and turned in one's hands.

One became angry, held it by the neck tightly and commanded it to sit. But each time one pressed its backside down and said 'sit,' it got up again immediately. And then one hit it. First just a gentle blow to the snout. A blow, which one was actually shocked that one could deliver. A further blow. Then two more. And the kitten was powerless. Was held by the tail, so it couldn't run back. With claws and teeth that were too small to cause any real damage.

Suddenly one regretted, and began almost to cry. Wanted to comfort and hold it. But the kitten just wanted to get away, so one let it go and shouted sorry after it.

Ran out into the kitchen and found some pâté, divided it up into little portions and poured milk out into a little saucer. Called again and knew that it had hidden itself away in the room.

Closed the door, so it couldn't slip away and smelt faeces.

Looked under the bed and saw the kitten sat right up against the wall. Further along the skirting lay its smelly little offering.

Suddenly felt angry again. Furious. Fetched a coat hanger from the mother's cupboard and squeezed one's way in under the bed, so as to be able to reach it.

The kitten ran out, but the only other place to hide was the corner by the door.

Fetched a belt. There was no way back now. It thought it was so sweet. But the only thing it was good at was crapping on the floor and running away and not let itself be petted.

The belt was attached to its throat and tightened. But the kitten was too small for the belt to throttle it, and when it just hung and kicked out into thin air with its large wet eyes and refused to die, the only thing to do was to give up.

Opened a window, to air the room, get rid of the

stench and threw the kitten out, hard, at the ground. Watched curious and scared to see what would happen to it.

The clump turned in the air and landed in a heap on the ground in a little play area. And that's where it stayed, quiet and crumpled.

One removed the faeces and returned to the window. The kitten was gone. Gone, like the mother and the big brother and everybody else in the entire world. Laid down in the bed and cried oneself to sleep.

But things went well in school, even though one was often late.

The girls had started to grow breasts and the boys hit and slapped anything that moved. Especially the girls, whilst discussing genital hair and French kissing.

Played 'Truth or Dare?', played football and did homework. Never quite managed to get it done, and only very rarely on time.

The exercise books one had used to write stories in had been chucked out together with the colourful drawings of huge medieval battles and deadly fighter planes in air combat during the Second World War. By accident. But when the kids had left and gone far away – one was oneself hospitalised at that point – the mother felt that it was time for a good clean out. A clean out where all the old stuff got chucked out. That was for the best, she felt. Like a fresh start.

Suspected that the mother had probably read the

words *cock* and *cunt* in the exercise books, and war was never a good thing. She never understood the bigger picture. The bigger stories. So big that one couldn't contain them. They took up too much space.

Instead one spent one's time going to the cinema and stealing from shops. Sweets, magazines, everything. Especially porn. Not so much for oneself, but for the kids at school who were that bit older. They got them for half price. But ... one kept the best ones anyway.

Ran around with Mads and planned a big job. Mads, who was the same age and lucky and lived in a house with a TV in his room. The big jobs.

And one drew, and Mads he nodded. A shoe shop, where there was bound to be money. There always was in the places you least expected to find it.

But, of course, it turned out that there was no money, just shoes and packaging.

A frustrating fact that led one to knock over and smash up the stock, before setting fire to everything and running off.

And when it wasn't robbery it was cars. Preferably sports cars.

One of them was too fast. So fast that one lost control and crashed through a hedge and had to leave the car in a garden.

The rest of the time was just spent wandering the streets in the town centre. Preferably drunk and always noisy - the owner of the entire cursed world.

Somewhere inside there was still something that hurt

too much to give one the strength to really break out. To really riot. And in reality one would actually rather sit in the club or in the park by the lake.

Would have rather been doing that when one broke the head of an innocent, chubby bloke in his sixties. A man one knew well actually. He'd been there before. One knew his habits. Even though he'd only recently moved in. The whore.

She had just finished her blow job or anal bondage or whatever. At any rate a red light was on in the living room. A certain sign that she was open for business. That was obvious.

A prostitute one had quickly learnt to keep an eye on from the living room. Mostly for the sake of the excitement and because she often gave convincing blow jobs. Her mouth and the hand with the rattling arm rings.

But not that evening. Not that evening, where one had spotted the regular returning customer who always turned up in his big expensive car. With his cock stiff and his hair swept back.

Not that evening, where the modest car park's lighting was out of order and was now in almost total darkness.

The customer threw his jacket on to the back seat, sat himself behind the wheel and fished out a cigarette. Smoked and sat taking notes. Making up accounts as usual. There was plenty of time to creep up to him. Up to the jacket and the wallet one knew would be lying on the back seat. It was just a question of opening the door, grabbing the gear and pegging it. Just as Mads had described it.

The man took a final drag on his cigarette and glanced, probably habitually, in his rear-view mirror. At any rate he'd spotted one crawling along on all fours.

The man puffed and blew and swore as he tried to get out of the car.

One caught Mads' eye, but he just continued to stare and nodded seriously.

Was trapped. Didn't want to let down a friend, and didn't want to stay. One got up. Without a word.

The man was already halfway out of his car and had the door smashed against his shins. And then. Then came the rock. The weapon one had agreed to threaten with if it became necessary. And in this case a threat was called for.

But one never remembered to threaten. Just to hit. Again and again. And it was fun while it lasted, great fun. It tickled his stomach and took the edge off his terror. Up to the point when the man stopped grunting and swearing but just lay down across the front seats. As if he'd felt tired and had decided to take a nap. Not nearly as noisy and dramatic as one had expected. And yet the nausea came.

Began to shake. Couldn't stop himself.

The blood covered the man's eyes and smelt of metal. Cuts all over him.

One threw away the rock and dried one's hands in

one's trouser legs and sped off. Never noticed the rock's fall, or saw it break in two.

But the money, five hundred kroner bills and two fifties, made things feel much better, at least until it was time for Mads to go home. Until one was alone again. And it was then. On that evening just then, that one realised that one would never use violence again. That one neither would or could. Without a doubt.

Still alone. Praying to God, promised, that one would never do anything wrong again, if just God would bring one someone, someone so one didn't have to be alone any more. One thought of one's mother and listened for footsteps on the stairs. If she could just be there till one fell asleep. So one could hold her hand or hear her breathing. The calming sound of her breath.

But God didn't hear one. Because one had only just entered one's teens and already had a reputation as one of the neighbourhood's worst tearaways. And the girl in class had told him that thieves were damned and would be crucified.

One sought comfort by thinking about something else. By thinking of one's brother. The brother who travelled to other countries. The brother who in his letters had described precisely how he drank and danced and befriended beautiful chocolate-coloured women.

Black as night, with pink tongues and delicate pink cunts – one was old enough to be told the truth now. One couldn't really decide whether one wanted to hear the details. And yet. The thing about the women was dirty enough. Though it wouldn't have mattered if the brother had kept the pink pussies to himself. But the descriptions of the many boat trips, the harbour and heaving hurricanes. That was exciting. Hurricanes that were so powerful that just a single squall could haul containers off into the depths. Containers that, because of a lack of space in the hold, were roped down with steel wire on deck, and which were now washed overboard as if they were just made of paper.

The brother took the cheap container ships to save money, so he wrote. And he helped out if they needed a hand. And they often did, or so it seemed. In most of his letters the brother had just left one ship for another.

And one dreamed ...

Christian was drunk. He had nothing to get up to, and in any case he didn't care. He drank all day.

When, late in the evening, he popped out after yet another pack of cigarettes, he bought a couple of extra six packs as well.

It was going to be a good night. A really good night with loud music, plenty of fags and lots of beer.

# 6

The script, the film. Once again Christian was beginning to doubt. The doubt that left him unable to act. The doubt that left him unable to do anything except feel scared. Scared to go out. Scared to move. Scared to talk to anyone. All that was left was the dream. The dream that kept him going, helped him get over the worst of it. The dream of success and recognition for his masterpieces. The dream of a life like Francis Ford Coppola's, for example.

Wasn't it Bille August, who once said that the day there was no longer a limousine waiting for you, you knew something was wrong. But there would always be limousines waiting for Christian. It was just a matter of time. A matter of the sign from God, and of timing.

When Christian looked around him, he was still shocked over how much utter rubbish was made. So many films that no-one ever saw, except all the Hollywood crap.

It was all for laughs. Yep. Not for thinking about. All to be consumed, devoured, swallowed, gorged on. And then just as thoughtlessly farted, shat and pissed out again.

Christian cursed and despised them all. Both the people who made them and those who came to watch them. The same thought came back to him again and again: If only he had a chance he'd show them. Then the whole *world* would see.

But no-one seemed to see. No-one seemed to see his way. No-one seemed to believe in him.

Christian had now been everywhere: To the Danish Film Institute, to film producers, to friends. Those, at any rate, who called themselves friends.
But everyone just laughed behind his back. And he knew they thought he was talentless. He knew they derided him in the same way, that he derided them. He knew it. He could see it in their eyes.

At the annual *Robert* awards party in the Imperial cinema, a sort of Danish Oscars, Christian happened, by chance, to run into one of the really big film moguls. He was just standing there gulping back glasses of red wine. One after the other.
They only knew each other from a pitch the mogul had attended, and Christian was more than a little happy at the fact that it was the mogul who acknowledged him and not the other way around. It was a question of having a feel for the details. And Christian had that. Without question he had that. A sense for details and logistics. Two key ingredients when you were making films.
The mogul was a bit drunk, but was sober enough for a conversation and could still think clearly. He asked Christian generally how he was doing, and whether he'd got any further with his project.
Christian had to admit that nothing had happened. The

Danish film industry was too small for a lie about an upcoming project to be sustainable for long. Anyway, it happened all the time. People on the periphery, like himself, and the more established names, again and again spun a story about all the wonderful things they were just on the point of bringing to life.

And then ... then the impossible happened. The sort of thing that only happened in films. The mogul did something amazing and unexpected. He believed in Christian's talent and was willing to give him a chance.

A chance?!

Yes, he'd give him a chance.

Finally the pieces were falling into place. And here of all places. In Denmark's biggest cinema, where his film would probably première. And at the Roberts awards party, where he would be showered with awards. It was a sign. It *had* to be a sign. It was *the* sign! Oh, God is great. *Thank-you, thank-you, thank-you, dear God.*

Christian could feel a couple of tears in his eyes and blinked. The world stood still. The sound of the clinking glasses and the noisy talk around them disappeared. He had finally been discovered. Had finally been recognised!

The film mogul continued. Offered Christian access to everything he had available. Everything. Facilities, equipment, editing. Even film. There was always a couple of cans left over from another production. The only thing he couldn't offer was money.

The sounds and the noise returned. As if through a long, long tube.

Somebody laughed. Christian turned quickly searching for the source of the noise. It sounded like one of his demons. It *was* a demon. Standing there in the middle of everything just laughing at him.

Someone dropped a beer and shouted *fuuck!*

The beer sprayed out onto the carpeted floor almost in slow motion.

Christian stared at the mogul through eyes that were screwed up tight. Shut his mouth. Ground his teeth together.

He should have known. Should have been able to see it coming. Of course. How stupid can you get, thought Christian. Arrogant bastards.

The cunt was just fucking standing there mocking him to his face. Pissing on him.

As if it wasn't clear. As if it wasn't perfectly clear to anybody. If Christian was going to make a film then it should be on the same terms as anybody else. As a paid screenwriter and director. And, of course, the mogul knew that. Anything else was reserved for amateurs and time-wasters. Perhaps something one could try out on new and unproven talents. But not on Christian?! Christian who was neither new or unproven, and who'd passed his apprenticeship long ago. He knew everything there was to know about making films.

Several of the directors he knew personally had never

so much as set foot on a film set – never. And they got bucket-loads of money, while Christian had *several* years of experience now.

Even though Christian had never actually directed a feature film that didn't mean he wasn't talented. And in any case, personal experience wasn't everything or totally necessary or anything. And now, when Christian had a script for a film finished and ready, he was to be dragged through it again, and humiliated one more time.

Why? Bille August could get money, Lars Von Trier and Susanne Bier could get money. Ole Bornedal and Thomas Vinterberg and Soeren Kragh-Jacobsen could get money.

They were humiliating him. Ridiculing him. Spitting on him. Trampling him under foot.

What a great story Christian would be able to tell when they met each other in the editing room, in the canteen or at Cannes, where of course, they all went each year in order to show off and mingle with even more famous film-makers from America. There'd be something to talk about all right ...

Christian was friendly but firm.

If the film was to be made it would be done *properly*. In other words with an artificially accumulated budget like all the others, prepared by a practised production manager, and with as much taken care of in-house as possible, so money could circulate internally. Money, government grants.

That's the way it was. That was the system. The entire film industry ran on handouts. It wasn't even the producers' own money.

Christian hadn't wasted his time at university. He knew the score. At any rate he knew just as much as if he had been to university.

The film mogul asked Christian if he didn't think he was setting his sights a little high.

He asked the question calmly and gently. Not angrily. And without a feeling of being insulted. Not accusingly. Just quizzically. Christian didn't know what to answer, and just coughed repeatedly.

"No, it's not that at all. I just want to be taken seriously."

The mogul ignored his comment and said that Christian wasn't that far from being just another dreamer.

"Do you follow football? ... Have a look around. Can you see how many people there are going around with their hands up celebrating even though they've yet to score a goal. There are plenty of them that never get a sniff of the goal. Plenty of them aren't even on the team."

"... ... ... I need to go to the bathroom."

When Christian came out again, he avoided the area he'd been in previously, and moved to the other end of the bar. Emptied glass after glass and could only bring himself to growl at Joakim, who suddenly emerged from the crowd. He'd forgotten that they'd agreed to meet up in the foyer.

Joakim didn't mind much. He was in a hurry to get back to his new girlfriend. He made his way back out into the throbbing mob and disappeared, as he tried to shield the two glasses of wine he was balancing in his hands.

Suddenly Christian couldn't take it any more. He needed to get away. Out. Needed to breathe.

At first he thought of taking a bus, but the thought of passengers was too much for him. He hailed a taxi instead and asked the driver to drop him off on the corner. Next to the little newsagents where he normally bought beer outside normal opening hours.

On the way up the stairs to his flat he felt almost as if he was being chased, and he was on the verge of panic by the time he finally managed to get the key in the door. The bag of beers bashed dangerously against the door frame as he stepped quickly inside and shut the door behind him. He heaved his jacket off and threw it to the floor and almost ran to the stereo to put some music on. Within a second his trembling hand had reached into the bag after a beer. He sat down and emptied it. Then he fetched a glass from the kitchen and started on the next one. Finally he felt calm. He let the music flow over his body and considered going away. Travelling, just for a while. But then again, hadn't he travelled enough? Christian remembered how, when he'd had to go to boarding school, he'd cried to himself. Inside.

One year at boarding school. Not because one was difficult, but more for one's own good. So that there were some adults around and, of course, for the mother's sake. Her life was so hard. She took pills every now and then, but she still needed to be herself. And, of course, she was working most of the time. And that wasn't something a boy should have to see.

The boyfriend was hardly ever around when the mother was in the flat. And when he did finally show up, he always just sat silently and chain smoked in a corner. He didn't want to interfere in the way other people raised their kids, as he said.

So he was sent to boarding school. A boarding school where he really developed a taste for girls. Girls and film. And when one wasn't occupied with dreams of beating the others at athletics and receiving the entire school's accolades, one dreamt of girls.

One afternoon one was sitting in the common room watching TV with the others. Had at one point been alone. Changed the channel to one of the German stations and saw an award ceremony. There. Right there on screen. It was there, right there as the audience had stood up, and the applause rang round the room that one first felt the belief that it could actually be done. That the pictures in one's head could actually materialise, be realised.

As he watched, he caught a glimpse of a figure at the limit of his field of vision. Saw that it was a girl. That it was Helene. Didn't dare return her look and fixed his eyes on the screen instead. Girls. These peculiarly attractive individuals which in one way or the other were so foreign.

One evening one was invited over to the girls' annex, and even though it wasn't allowed, one crept in under the duvet of the long-limbed one. Helene. A girl with a stutter, and, who for that reason, seemed less intimidating than the others. Not that she wasn't very attractive. She was just more calm and introverted. Something that in some way attracted him.

She didn't waste time though. Told one to take of one's pants. One turned one's back and did so. Wanted to hide the spots of urine. Was in too much of a hurry and tripped around with one foot stuck in the elastic. Making a noise.

She hushed him and laughed.

One felt that her body was warm, and for a long time one just lay pressed up against her. Then one felt a certain impatience. A sort of eagerness to move on, whilst, for one's own part one was just interested in lying there and being allowed to hold and be held.

She pressed one's hand between her legs, whilst she started to feel around with her own. And, at first, it was wonderful. Right up to the point where she pushed one's hand right up in her. Up to a place that was both warm and sticky.

One ripped back one's hand in distaste and was already on one's way out of the bed again.

She asked if one liked it.

Didn't know what to answer. One was too shy.

She took hold of one's hand and pulled it down under the duvet again.

She was only just adult, was what one thought as one reluctantly did as she wanted.

She rolled onto her back and asked one to lie down on top of her. One wasn't that stupid. But one wasn't in any state to continue. The thought of the dark warm place between her legs was still an unpleasant memory. A memory of something naughty. At any rate a memory of something wet and unpleasant. A thought that suddenly gave birth to a violent anger which extended to everything about the girl. Suddenly one hated her.

Helene took hold of one's cock and tried to guide it up inside herself. She grunted. It sounded so fake.

One took hold of her hands and pulled them harshly away, but if Helene was upset she didn't show it. Didn't say anything as one crept out again. But one wasn't invited back.

And now there she was again. Standing there in the periphery of the TV room.

"I, I, I for-, for-, forgive you. Because, because, because you are so special."

Even though one thought she was more than strange, it was the saving of one's evening. One's whole life was lifted up, up, up in the air, and if they were never boyfriend and girlfriend, they were definitely there or there about.

And one was satisfied, because the brother would soon be home, and with the brother one could handle anything.

And then. Then they came, a double whammy. Two white envelopes. One an airmail letter, the other just an ordinary one.

The brother had decided to stay abroad for one more year, maybe more. It was still fun. And there was so much to see, so much to do. But he thought about one a lot, one should know that.

The other letter, a letter with the mother's neat handwriting on the front, just contained the usual nonsense about life with work and the pleasure she took in her big boys. Never a word about the daughter who had disappeared long ago and forever. The mother finished off with a little by the way to the effect that one had decided that he was to remain at the boarding school for the rest of his school life.

One never found out who *one* was.

Instead, one wrote a death notice. '*A good and loving brother. A good and loving mother. Thanks for everything.*' Then one framed the text by drawing a large black cross around it.

# 7

All Christian needed to do now was to write a conclusion and edit the story. Then it would be ready. Ready for the company which had previously expressed an interest. The biggest. The company with the range and the capacity. With the progressiveness. That dared to take chances.

And Christian read the professional literature. Spent time, once more, in the city's film libraries and on the Internet. Just for safety's sake. Just so as things could be done properly.

And Christian rewrote and corrected and cut. He read aloud and played the characters to the hall mirror. He went up and he went down. He gave the scenes colours, so that they could reflect the emotional tone. He wrote transport scenes. He thought camera angles and camera movements. He thought lights and filters. He thought lenses and perspectives. He thought dolly versus crane. Sound and music. Budgets and team sizes. Location and casting. Makeup and costumes.

And he wrote up. And he wrote down. And wrote notes. And was one with his film. He *was* the film. But most important of all was the story. The story which was greater than him. Greater than life. Greater than the universe.

Was it worth telling? Was it touching enough? Was it plausible enough? And he said yes to it all and was happy. This story was one they *could not* say no to.

Because, as always, he had put his whole heart and soul into it. One thousand percent.

And he would be happy the day the letter arrived. The day they told him that they would buy the script. The day they wanted him. The day when all the defeats could be turned to success. To a fabulous victory. And not just for him. No, no. The company would also benefit. And he would be one of the boys. And he'd be allowed to make more. All the ridicule and the insults would be forgotten. His too. He could forgive. They had to give him that. They *would* give him that.

Christian refused to ask himself why they had chosen to return his script. He just put it to one side and started reading the long letter. The letter in which the company's consultant acknowledged that yes, Christian was a good writer, BUT ...

And there was always a but. Always that fucking pathetic little word, that could kill everything.

Had they never taught them that they should never write BUT in a letter like that? And what the fuck did they know anyway?

BUT the story was still far too unstructured and incoherent for it to be made in its current form. And in any case there were elements of dramatic progression lacking. However, Christian was welcome to continue working on it and to submit it again at a later date.

At this point Christian went blank. As always happened. He just sat and stared emptily out of the window for hours at a time. Could hardly get it together to drag himself over to the newsagent's to buy food or beer. Could hardly bring himself to *eat* food. All he could do was sit and reflect on how meaningless it all was. How utterly without purpose. And curse himself. Curse his pathetic thoughts, hopes and dreams. What the fuck had he expected? For, if truth be told, he was actually worth jack shit. He was less than nothing. Worthless, talentless. A fool. A jerk.

Most of all, however, he cursed the pusillanimous decision makers. The small, the conniving, the really talentless. All those who, like him, had dreamt, but had compromised and ended up working as consultants.

And it was the same everywhere you looked. The reviewers in the papers, the film consultants at the Film Institute, the lecturers at the film school, the Minister of Culture and the civil servants, the film producers and their ridiculous big-titted secretaries. All those who weren't *with* Christian were against him. That's the way it was. And now everyone was against him.

But someone had to stand up and be counted. Someone had to dare to take risks and experiment. It was just a question of finding a path. Because everything he turned his hand to seemed to end up dead in the water, and it was always because of incompetent people in key positions, he thought.

The telephone rang. It was the manager of the property where Christian cleaned the stairs. They wanted to have a talk with him. Today, if he could manage it.

Christian sensed that something was up, and his

fears were confirmed straight away as he entered the manager's office. They were going to have to let him go, as part of a rationalisation process they had decided to employ a cleaning company that would be taking care of all the properties.


"Cuuut! Okay, I think it would be good if we could close the set."

The First AD nods his agreement.

"Everyone apart from the DP, the first AC and sound can go and take a break. Come on people let's move. We still have a lot to do here."

The first AD begins herding the team off the set as he gather the clapboard up.

"I'll do it, okay?"

The clapper loader nods, of course ...

"Sound!"

"Speed!"

"Camera!"

"Camera's rolling!"

"117, take seven!"

*Smack!*

"Set!"

"Action!"


It was an advertising job for a beer brand. A studio shoot. Again. A couple of days outside would have been good. His bad mood and low energy levels would have benefitted from being outside, instead of spending two long days in a hot film studio. With cables and lamps and running around working.

Christian looked around him whilst he tried to chat with the makeup artist. They were ready and all they were waiting for now were the final camera adjustments. Christian spotted an unfamiliar face. A production assistant. A woman.

He asked around discretely. No-one else seemed to know her.

A woman in her mid-twenties, really quiet, he thought.

Christian noticed that she avoided the light and always ensured that she kept to the shadows. He couldn't help his curiosity and completely forgot his bad mood.

Christian approached carefully. At the table with the coffee and cake and sweets and juice. Said hello, told her his name and what he did around the set. She answered Natasha. Quiet and a bit shy. That she was new here. The only person she knew was the production manager.

They had no further conversation during the rest of the day. Though they exchanged glances and smiled cautiously. She seemed somehow so vulnerable. Not that she didn't do her job. Not that she seemed weak. Just vulnerable. Something in her gaze betrayed it.

Christian couldn't sleep. He tossed and turned. Began

to play with himself, just to take the edge off the worst of the tension. Couldn't come, got tired and gave up. Finally fell asleep but woke several times during the night.

Next day he spent more time with her. Asked her what she did, when she wasn't making films.
Natasha said she was a student. That she was reading film studies at university.
Oh, that was funny. Christian had done that too. But she probably shouldn't spread it around too much. If word got out about his academic background, it might make it difficult for him to find work.
Natasha shrugged her shoulders.
Did she agree or disagree? Or was she just indifferent?
During lunch he sat opposite her. Asked if it was okay. Asked if the principal was still there. Whether there were any new lecturers.
Natasha answered yes to one thing and another, but changed the subject and asked a question about the director of photography.
Karl Braghe and the Swedish director sat at a remote table, away from the others, with the client and the ad agency.
Braghe was one of the best. If not *the* best. Had, it seemed, been making films since he was a kid. Had won tons of awards. Was quiet and calm. Very friendly. Not arrogant like you'd expect. Loved working with bits of mirror and little bits of styrofoam and, in

collaboration with the gaffer he could always produce fantastic lighting. And when that happened everyone just stepped back and let them get on with it. Only one of the lighting assistants stuck around. Sucking up the respect and providing assistance where he could.

Lunch was over.

The first AD came in making a racket as usual. Natasha scraped off the last of the food on her plate.

"If you're up for it, we could go and see a film together?"

Christian waited for her reaction.

She looked at him without answering. As if perplexed.

Christian went off disappointed.


"Check the gate."

The first AC checked the film mechanism in the camera for foreign bodies to make sure that the exposed film was okay.

"Clean gate."

Everyone was already in the process of clearing up.

"It's a wrap! Thanks everyone!"

Christian rolled up some cables.

"When should we say?"

Natasha stood with her hands in her back pocket. With a little turn of her hips. As if she was already on her way somewhere.

"Err ... now? I mean it's already getting late. We could go and get something to eat, and then head off to the cinema afterwards?"

"I'd like to just pop home first. Shall we meet at "Café Edge"? Around 8ish?"

The gaps in their conversation were far from unpleasant, in fact they brought calm and reflection. Time to study the cutlery and the food, time to look at the other guests and to analyse Natasha's body language.

Natasha, who grew up near Fredensborg, just north of Copenhagen, as she said. With rhododendrons, ferns, elder and forsythia. With a greenhouse and floral trellis and a herb garden. With a cat and rabbits and an elderly lady's bicycle. With breakfast in bed and songs on your birthday.

Natasha, who lived in a hall of residence alone. A friend had recently dragged her along to work as an extra, and afterwards, Natasha had given the production manager her number. If they ever needed an assistant, they could just call Natasha, she'd be happy to help.

Three weeks later the female production manger called and offered her a production assistant job. She felt that they got on well, and the more women in the film industry the better.

Natasha smiled. The green eyes ... The blue jeans, the black sparse jersey. The blonde hair. The round cheeks. The full hips. The flat sandals. The greying broken molar amongst pearly white teeth.

Christian began to talk about what he was doing right now. That he was planning to travel. Just to get away from it all for a bit. To get a bit of distance to things. Then he talked about the lecturers at the faculty. Not much, but enough to make an impression, he thought. Which ones were laughable, which were cool and so on.

He talked about all the people he'd studied with who went around with ambitions of becoming a film director – closet ambitions, and how ridiculous they actually were. Just think, what was the point in *studying* films instead of *making* films. What on earth did that help? The best you could hope for was to become a film history researcher, teach other disdainful Fellini's or maybe make it into Film School.

But there was no reason to feel disappointed, if they had dreams of studying at the Film School. Because, there wasn't much worth dreaming about there. All the Film School projects Christian had worked on or heard about from colleagues had, without exception, been completely talentless and pretentious. No, practical real world experience. Professional experience. With professional people. Anything else was a waste of time. And when it came down to it, you could practise all you wanted. If you were talentless it wouldn't make any difference.

The Film School types were hopeless when it came to the point. They didn't really get their hands dirty at all, just learnt a lot about artistic concepts. But when it was time for them to start their obligatory film projects, where they took it in turns to be production manager, runners, and so on, they came unstuck. Because it was suddenly obvious that they hadn't got a clue.

Of course, they tried to say to themselves that it was all just for experience's sake, and that they really ought to have people to do that sort of thing for them. Ha!

But, one left them alone of course. Left them to their illusion.

Then the "unit production manager" would make a couple of calls to people who were on their way up. People like Christian.

People, who'd actually worked as a grip assistant or a lighting assistant, could get to work as a real grip or gaffer, if they worked for nothing on a Film School project. And who wouldn't want to do that?

And then they booked equipment by trying the same trick: We're from the film school. We're cool. Help us out now, and we'll remember you when we make our first film.

But when they actually started recording it all fell to the ground. Where was the production plan, the shooting lists or the storyboard – you can't make a film without them, can you? – and where were the logistics? No, not a clue about anything other than that they were an artist.

Natasha said nothing.

Christian coughed. Suddenly insecure. Afraid he might have frightened her off.

"That's seems very one-sided to me. How about qualifying it a bit?"

Christian beat a retreat. Fought and dragged and pulled with a will that he didn't understand himself. He tried to smooth things over without losing face. Without losing status. Even insisted on paying the bill when they left.

The film was okay.
Natasha sat most of the time with her arms folded across her chest. She seemed tired.
Outside on the street she just stood there watching while Christian unlocked his bicycle.
"I'm feeling lonely right now. Do you want to come back with me?"
Before he'd dared to react she walked over to him and put her arms around him.
Her hair smelt of vanilla. She was warm.
Christian tried, overcome and surprised, to lean his bike somewhere, but it fell and knocked into the other ones. He let it lie.

They didn't talk much. Just rode side by side. Christian was nervous. He was unable to relax. Felt, with creeping desperation that he had to do something. And why didn't she say something? Said that he was probably going to go to the states and visit his brother. But when she didn't ask him about it, he let it lie. He looked at her out of the corner of his eye. She didn't seem very uneasy. Maybe it was just him. He tried to relax.

The hall of residence surrounded by lilacs.

She kissed him. In her own quiet way. Took her time, really took her time.

Christian stood there feeling tense. Awkward, pressed up against the desk in the little room. Felt the fear. Not the usual, stage fright.

"Why don't you take a bath?"

She asked him as if she was merely talking about a cup of coffee.

He stared into the sharp gaze of an eagle on the wall. A little black and white postcard image. Hanging side by side with the others. A tropical island and a naked violinist.

Natasha began undressing him. Then it all got too much for him. He drew away into a corner, where he could undress on his own.

He heard her arranging things in the bathroom. Expected her to come and visit him in the shower. She didn't.

She lay there waiting for him. On her side, with her head resting on one arm. Looking at him. Unashamedly.

Christian felt shy and nervous. He grabbed a corner of the duvet. She pushed it to one side. A wave of warm air streamed through the room. A smell of woman.

He lay down next to her. Let a hand run down her back and let it rest like a bowl on her buttock.

She turned around and pulled the duvet around her, as she pushed his legs apart. Kneeling up.

Christian wanted to get up. Wanted to touch her breasts, but she didn't let him. Avoided his hands and pushed him gently but firmly back onto the bed.

He could feel a sort of pulse in his solar plexus. And lay there feeling embarrassed by his lack of an erection.

She kissed his neck. His cheek. His mouth. His cheek and neck again. Slowly.

Christian couldn't take much more of this. He reached up again to grab her. And was pushed back once more.

He drew breath heavily and resigned himself to his fate. She generated calm. Unusual calm.

And Natasha carried on. The pulse moved from his diaphragm and worked its way down. The deep kisses became more frequent, as she neared his stomach. Moving around his prick.

Christian felt the pressure of her hands on his thighs. Just above the knees. And began to grow, slowly.

She took him into her mouth. Felt his tension and put a hand on his chest.

He relaxed. Relaxed like never before and accepted.

She smiled at him and lay up against him. With her head on his chest. Christian was broken. On the point of crying. And the world was simple and light and awake.

The morning was great. Natasha slept.

An overwhelming devotion ran through him. He crept close to her. Lay against her back and was completely happy. The feeling was so complete and so different he could have screamed. Felt the need to shout. To do something.

She grumbled in a friendly way and found his hand with hers. Moved it to her breast and let her own hand rest on top of it. They fell asleep again.


It became days of toing and froing between his home and hers. Nights of red wine and talking. Love and dreams. She asked him to visit the doctor and get himself tested. And everything was fine. And Christian found himself lying between her legs. Discovered that it was wonderful, that it was Natasha. That he liked to please her. He was so much in love that he could hardly bare it. They were such a good match, they talked so well, made love so well.

Natasha asked him whether they should go travelling together. Visit his brother, perhaps. It happened one evening when she suddenly remembered what he had said that first night. Didn't he live in the States? What did he do anyway? At first Christian had been evasive. Then she'd asked if it was a secret. No, no it wasn't but ... then, reluctantly, he'd told her all about him. As succinctly as possible. Without making anything of the big deal. The big deal that, of course, aroused her interest. So Natasha pressed him to travel. And Christian was evasive. Not now. Not yet, when they'd just got to know each other. Christian felt peculiarly dispirited.

"Why not? It's cheap at the minute."

She had the money. For a week anyway.

"It'd be great! Give him a call, say you're bringing your girlfriend."

Then Christian became irritable and was against the whole thing. Against it because he hadn't seen his brother for so long. Against it because Natasha would probably be bored half to death and would just feel that she'd wasted loads of money.

But Natasha didn't give up so easily.

"Come on, Christian. Call him. It'd be a blast. I've never been to the States. And to go to Hollywood - wow!"

Christian gave up and went next door to call his brother .

She heard him mumble from the living room. Sprang enthusiastically out of bed and stormed in and caught him round the waist.

"Ah, yeah okay. See you. Bye."

Christian put down the phone and told her that his brother wasn't in the States at the minute. Actually he was in London doing a commercial.

"Cool. Let's got to London instead. It'll be cheaper too."

But what about her exams? She'd need to revise, wouldn't she?

"I've got plenty of time and it doesn't have to be more than a couple of days. There are cheap flights from Copenhagen on Thursdays. They only cost 5-600

Kroner."

They shouldn't reckon on being able to stay with his brother. He'd just talked to her about it. About his girlfriend the model who'd already complained repeatedly that he spent too much time talking to Christian.

"Well, we can just find a cheap hotel. And we can do a bit of shopping. And see the city. It's a great place. I've been there loads of times. It'll be fantastic, lets got to London!"

Christian just shrugged his shoulders, but Natasha didn't notice. She ran over to the computer and fired up the Internet. Found the airline and booked their flights and hotel in under twenty minutes.

"Cuuut! Much, much better. One more time and we'll be there ... Just push him right to the edge. That was great!"

"Sound!"

"Speed."

"Camera!"

"Camera's rolling!"

"117, take eight!"

*Smack!*

"Set!"

"Aaand action!"

The airline didn't serve food on the flight so they were both starving by the time they reached their hotel: 'Palace Court', in Bayswater, just ten minutes from the tube.

A little, quiet hotel, where two narrow staircases connected the various floors.

The room was small. There was just enough room for a bed under a large window, an occasional table, a little wardrobe in the corner, a fourteen inch telly on the table – and a bathroom.

They divested themselves of their luggage and went looking for a place to eat.

The area around Moscow Road and Princes Square was full of restaurants. There were lots of Greek ones, but there were also Japanese, Libyan and Italian. The most difficult thing was choosing.

They opted for a little Thai restaurant and ate their lunch completely alone – they were the only customers. Drank *Tiger* beer and held hands across the table and the dripping wax. And everything was romantic and lovely.

Back at the hotel they continued their discussion from the restaurant about the rest of the trip. About shopping and wandering the streets, and, of course, when they should visit the brother.

It was now Natasha who was the active one. Planning. Finding the best route, and sorting out when and where. First they'd go there and do that and then ...

But they wouldn't be able to fit all that in, said

Christian. And it wasn't as if it was that important. And they had time for each other and the city, just to hang out and be themselves.

They shared a can of beer whilst they made love. She rode him hard with one hand on his testicles and the other on the beer. Drank and rode, drank and rode. Bubbling and spraying.

He licked beer from her nipples, whilst his fingers toyed with her.

They laughed together, let beer be beer and raised their tempo. They quickly turned manic, and Christian was beside himself, whilst Natasha broke down as soon as she had had her orgasm.

Christian hadn't quite gone all the way, but didn't do anything about it. He wasn't even frustrated. He wasn't even in pain, like he normally was, when he didn't come.

Natasha crept in under the duvet, kissed his shoulder and quickly fell asleep. Christian just lay there staring emptily at the ceiling.

They wandered. Up through *Hyde Park*. It was hot. Humid. Talked about what to see and what to do.

"Why don't you call your brother? You must be looking forward to seeing him. Maybe we could go and see him now."

Christian didn't answer, just sat on a bench and stared out into the park. Not a word. Closed off from the world.

Natasha asked him what was wrong. Kissed his hair. Christian shook his head.

"Are you afraid to see him?"

He lit up.

"Absolutely! Yes."

"I can understand that. Shall I call him?"

"No, no. Don't do that. Just give me a moment ... I'll call him, I'll do it."

Natasha stood up smiling.

"How about a little wander?"

"Sure, lets!"

Christian got up quickly. Gripped her hand. Kissed it. And pulled her along with him.

Oxford Street, Soho, down Regent Street and through Little China. On to Covent Garden.

They sat themselves somewhere, and Christian grabbed a mango juice whilst Natasha sat with a cola and ate a baked potato.

"I'll be back in a minute."

"Where are you going?"

Christian found a Boots, and bought some paracetamol. He'd had a headache since they'd arrived.

They didn't seem to help. He went back and found Natasha.

They took a number 15 to *St. Paul's Cathedral*. Went on the tour up through the whispering gallery and had a good look at London. They separated, but met again under the dome, after Christian had looked for her in the crypt.

Another number 15 and they were at *Tower Bridge* and the *Tower of London*.

They sat on a bench and looked across the bridge before crossing.

Everything costs money so they avoided the Tower and the drawbridge. Bought sweets on the waterfront and looked through an estate agent window at the price of flats. Just for the sake of it. Who knew, one day maybe they could afford one ...

The flats were nice, but they ended up agreeing that they faced the wrong way. The sun would shine into the bedroom in the morning not the living room.

They recrossed the bridge and decided to head back to their hotel.

Christian still had a killer headache. He tried to sleep it off. It didn't help.

Natasha wrote postcards and drank beer while Christian watched TV. Something about an execution in the States, someone who had evidently killed one hundred and sixty eight people.

They took a shower and went back into town looking for somewhere to eat. Got some air and fell out.

Christian thought Natasha was drinking too much, whilst Natasha thought that made them quits, given Christian's consumption of cigarettes.

"You smoke too for god's sake!" was Christian's response.

"Yeah, and you drink beer."

"Not as much as you."

"And I don't *smoke* as much as you do."

Okay, this was absurd. Unnecessary. Of course she could drink if she wanted to – she was paying – and of course he could smoke if he wanted to - just so long as he opened the window.

They laughed and that took the heat out of their mood. Now they stood trying to make a decision. Greek or fish and chips. Ended up not choosing either, ended up in the '*Art Café*' on Bayswater Road where Christian ate lasagne, and Natasha tucked into scampi. Then he sat sipping his red wine. Seemed to be pulling himself together.

Natasha made a noise by running her finger round the rim of the glass.

"... Don't you want to know where he is?"

"Actually, I was just thinking the same."

Christian got up and went over to the bar to ask if there was a phone he could use.

Natasha sat considering a dessert and studied the menu for the third or fourth time.

Christian came back and sat down quickly.

The brother was working out at Pinewood Studios. In Iver Heath.

"Well, let's just head out there?"

"They probably won't let us in."

"I thought you agreed something or other with him."

"He was busy. They were doing the *dailies*, so ..."

"That's a big job. Wasn't it a commercial?"

"Yeah, but it's part of a whole series. For Coca Cola, I think."

"Well we could just tell them who we were there to see?"

Christian turned aggressive. Thought it was childish. You didn't just head off out to some film studio. Just to get a whiff of celebrity or something, and Christian wasn't going to risk being taken for some stupid fan. No way.

But Natasha stuck to her guns. She thought it was all just in his head. If you were going there to visit someone who happened to work at the studio, then it was something completely different.

Even though Christian seemed both angry and irritable he answered that *'no, of course she was right,'* in a fashion that was almost over friendly.


The sun shone over Bayswater. Spring had really come to London. The cherry trees had been in bloom for some time, and the last daffodils stood still erect, even though summer was just around the corner.

They took the tube to Paddington and on from Paddington to Uxbridge, changing trains a couple of times en route. At Uxbridge they had to take a taxi that took them the last bit of the way through a myriad of roundabouts.

The driver seemed to know what he was doing, so they said nothing when he drove right past the main entrance to the studios on Pinewood Road. A couple of minutes later he rolled to a halt in the expansive guest parking area.

"This should do it, mate. Timekeeper Gate."

Christian paid while Natasha waited impatiently.

After a bit of wandering back and forth in the car park to give Christian a chance to pull himself together, Natasha was still waiting for him. He found a cigarette, and walked over to her coughing.

"Are you okay?"

He nodded.

Natasha got hold of the security guard. They were here to visit a film director who was working on one of the sets. A Mr. Thomas Klerke.

The guard asked whether they knew where Mr. Clerke was filming. Or, at any rate, what he was working on.

Natasha looked at Christian, who just shrugged his shoulders. She thought it was Coca Cola.

"No, no. I didn't say that!"

Christian was right beside her just like that.

"I *thought*, it was Coca Cola. But I'm not sure."

Natasha looked at him. As if she was considering something. Talked to the guard again. Was there someone they could ask? Someone who might know. They'd just arrived. All the way from Denmark. It was supposed to be a surprise. Christian here was Thomas Klerke's brother.

The guard smiled and had a good look at them. He liked the look of Natasha. Really liked the look of her. He rang the stage manager. Asked for a director called

Thomas Clerke, but shook his head, he needed the name of the production.

And they didn't know that.

Then it was pretty much impossible. At any rate the stage manager couldn't help them. They could try the production coordinator.

The guard tried again. Asked his question, was put on hold and, was in luck. There was a Mr Clerke on the 007 set. A Mr. T. Clerke. A bestboy gaffer.

The guard thanked him and hung up. Started rummaging for a couple of guest passes.

Natasha was radiating enthusiasm.

"This is it Christian."

Christian threw away his cigarette.

"What?"

"I said this is it. Let's go visit him. He's working on the James Bond set."

"What?! Are you sure? I mean… it's Thomas *Klerke* we're talking about, right? The director."

"Go ask him yourself."

Christian went over to the guard. Asked a couple of quick questions. Questions that resulted in a couple more phone calls.

Which production was it?

They didn't know. All they knew was that it was a commercial, and that he wasn't a lighting guy – he was a director.

Christian's coughs now came between almost every word.

No. Sorry. Almost the only things in production at the minute were films, a lot of the sets were vacant and were just waiting for someone to let them. It was a bit of a dead period. There were only a couple of adverts: *Procter & Gamble* and *Ford*. And none of the directors were called Clerke. Were they sure they weren't shooting at Shepperton Studios?

Christian seemed relieved. Natasha shook her head in irritation. – "Didn't you say was working at Pinewood?"

"Yes."

"Well, he's not here is he?"

"No, evidently not."

"Doesn't that bother you? I mean, wasn't that why we came here?"

"No, no, no. That's why *you* came here."

Natasha stood for a while and thought things through.

"Shouldn't we ask about that guy working on the set?"

"Ask? What did you want to ask about?"

"Well, not ask exactly. Just find out if it was him."

Christian was more calm now.

"Well, it isn't. We just found that out. The bloke was a gaffer. And his name was spelt with a 'C'."

"They might have spelt it wrong? It would be a bit stupid to go all the way back to Copenhagen just because of that."

"They haven't made a mistake, Natasha. They

haven't."

"How can you be so sure?"

"Places like this, they don't make that kind of mistake. Definitely not with people's titles and surname. Trust me."

Christian suddenly seemed arrogant. Which was unlike him.

"Can't we ask the guard to call Mr. Klerke, with or without 'C'? Just to be on the safe side?"

"Be my guest ... it's not going to help though."

Stubbornly, Natasha went back to the guard. This time he let her make the call. Christian could hear her flirtatious voice and retreated out of earshot. Couldn't take hearing any more. Almost felt sorry for her.

Natasha walked over to him.

"Well, it wasn't him, of course."

Christian said nothing.

"What now? What should we do next?"

Christian went over to her and took her hand hesitantly. Caught her green eyes.

"Whatever, *I* don't care. He's not *my* brother. I just thought, it would have been fun to see the studios ... Aren't you a bit disappointed?"

"Yeah, but on the other hand, I hadn't really been counting on it. The man is really busy, and anything can have come up."

"He doesn't have a mobile?"

"No, no. Doesn't believe in them."

"That means you can only get hold of him in the

evening when he's at home or what?"

"Yeah, yeah. That's just the way he is."

"What about his hotel? And where did you call him yesterday? And on what number?"

"Just leave this to me will you. He's *my* brother."

"You haven't called him have you? You're too scared to meet him right."

"No ... ... You're right."

Christian looked the other way.

"Why didn't you just say so?"

Natasha kissed him gently on the forehead.

"Hey Christian, hey. For fuck's sake, it's okay."

Christian let himself fall into her arms.


Portobello Road. They wandered around, continued to Notting Hill Gate and took the tube to Waterloo Station. From there they took the tube to Hampton Court, changing at Surbiton.

The sun was shining from what was an almost cloudless sky.

Just taking their time and enjoying being tourists. They found their way to the castle, but thought it too expensive. Sat themselves on a bench in the huge well-tended garden and enjoyed the sunshine. Went to the labyrinth, where you had to pay to get in or have a student card, but they let them in on a child's ticket.

They found their way to the centre of the maze, exited again and wandered past the tea shop, where, of course, the prices were exorbitant.

Found a newsagent and bought a couple of sandwiches.

Sat down on a pontoon bridge by the river, were attacked by some hungry geese and swans and retreated to a bench by the roadside. They enjoyed the relaxed tempo, just feeling each other's presence and breathing the same air. And they had a great time anyway. Even though they didn't visit his brother.

During the final night in the hotel Christian awoke with a shout, whilst Natasha just mumbled in her sleep. It was one of the bad ones, and the anxiety was still there like a breathless knot in his chest. He got up and drank some of the whisky they'd bought in the airport. He was sweating heavily and had to open the window, breath the night air and have another drink.

The final night at the boarding school. The night that had been the worst of all. Where it all came to a head. The night he'd decided to kill himself. Kill himself. With his own hands. Put a stop to his accursed life. Why? It didn't make sense. Nothing made sense. Life made no sense. And one didn't want to go back. For there was nothing to go back to. No going back ever. Not to the empty flat. He'd rather kill himself.

One had completed one's schooling, one should be happy. Would be going back to the old familiar. To one's mates.

Huddled under the duvet. Freezing. And then, suddenly, they were there again. Stronger. And so much more terrifying than before. The noises. Silence pregnant with sound. And the fear, the sudden fear.

He coughed. Coughed again and again. And even though it was a disgusting habit, because it was so embarrassing one wanted to cry, it was something. Something to hold on to. A source of comfort.

The sound of his rasping voice quietened the sounds from the walls and the ceiling and the air around one. These whispers, so evil.

The night where the dark was overwhelming. The night where one fell asleep exhausted. After a furious and savage fight. Hoarse with a throat that was dry and sore. The night where one had cried as never before. The night where one had prayed as never before. The cursed night. The night that was so unfair.

One lay with flaming cheeks. But slept. They'd never been this close before. So close to driving one insane.

Sleeping and dreaming of an angel that flew down and sat itself by one's bed. An angel that told one not to be afraid. Because everything was going to be all right. Soon it would all be better.

One woke to see a woman riding past his window on a bicycle.

One returned to the big city. Without a school to go to, without a job and with no enthusiasm. Let one day follow the other. Let one's mum pay the bills. Tried to drink and smoke. Tried to revisit old friends and old habits. But couldn't. Didn't dare. Didn't want to. One was far too scared of losing one's mind. The last bit of one's self control. Was caught and couldn't escape. The anxiety was no worse, but no better, even though the noises seemed to have gone away.

One coughed. Coughed constantly. Built up rituals and compulsive behaviour to quell the fear, doors were checked each time they were locked, and the light was turned on to see if it was off.

Initially one found it irritating. For one knew only too well, deep inside, that it was just nonsense, so one corrected oneself. Told oneself off. But despite this, one couldn't help oneself.

Or there was the way one dealt with the cutlery and the cups and plates. And the tins and food and the shoes and clothes in the cupboard. Everything had to be in exactly the right place where one had decided it should be. All the handles had to point to the right. All the plates had to be trim with the shelf edge. All the cutlery had not just to be clean and placed in the middle of the drawer, but to be truly and totally clean and to be placed in exactly the right place in the drawer. Where dust and other impurities were removed as soon as they were spotted. Where hands were washed again and again.

And it helped to write and draw again. Now inspired by cinema films. Inspired by films on TV. And this time things were allowed to just lie there, till they accumulated. In piles, enormous massive piles, and in nit-pickingly particular order of course.

And when one was out it was good. Because it all seemed so clean and nice and safe somehow. One could relax more, be more oneself. One could talk like all the others. One could smile and, as a rule, be friendliness itself. When one wanted peace – if one felt oneself threatened – one just used one's newly acquired weapon: A way of looking dead ahead that prevented all the others from getting in one's way. It was very effective. One could move around unhindered without being afraid that anyone would speak to one when one didn't want them to. And on the occasions where one felt that things were on the point of going wrong, one just let one's gaze focus on a fixed point in the distance. A useful and stylish unapproachability. It was the best way one knew of. The strongest and most effective weapon against everything.

But one could anyway surprise oneself and look forward to getting home to one's work. Home to the text and the letters.

And life carried crazily on, until the mother informed one that she and the boyfriend were moving in together and that it was probably about time one found oneself a better place to live – one chose not to comment on the fact that the mother and the boyfriend had been living together for many years already.

The mother continued in the same vein, telling one that one was soon more than adult, and just look at the big brother and big sister who had moved out when they were just fifteen, and without her even having to ask them.

Not a word about the fact that she had moved out to a life where no-one could reach her. Where no-one really knew what she was up to or where she was. And one's fixed point was of no use. Not now where one suddenly was required to do something and be responsible for the rest of one's life. How was it one did things? Acted and took responsibility, made decisions and chose? It was all so impossible, and one was scared again. And the fear came storming back, like a herd of stampeding cattle. And one could do nothing. One was unable to act. How was it one did that sort of thing?

One feared and trembled. Wandered the streets. Sought and prayed to one's God. Prayed for a pointer, a direction.

Finally one found a solution. On the advice of one's neighbour. The neighbour one otherwise never met and never talked to. The only thing one knew was that she had a gay son.

A large woman, expansive and happy, Kaija Oestergaard, who suggested he ask at an office where they rented out rooms. The same place that her son had found a place – this last one chose to ignore.

A little cheroot smoking woman who administered a couple of small housing associations and some flats. And yes there were rooms to rent. Especially to quiet, young and well-behaved men. And she could see straight away that was just what one was.

The room had its own little balcony come terrace. Unnecessary really, since it was on the ground floor. The architect had probably just wanted things to match, thought Christian. It was black and white and airy. Twenty square meters and with its own shower-room.

Ulla Hulstrup, the overweight daughter of about forty, and *Mrs* Hulstrup lived on the top floor. The kitchen was only good for tea and hard-boiled eggs. One never found out why they hadn't made more out of it. Not that it mattered much. In time he bought himself a little fridge and a little mini-oven, that was just the right size for the space above the fridge. And it was good, and it was safe, and it was nice.

Also the evening in the shower when he'd heard her rummaging in the living room. And the next day when he was boiling an egg, and she just happened to need to wash the floor. The overweight, awkward and clumsy Ulla who otherwise never came down when he was home. That's the way it had been up till now at any rate. And on all fours.

He apologised for his own presence and promised to hurry, now that she evidently didn't want him to postpone it.

First of all she'd crawled round in the corner with her back to him in some blue and white striped cotton get up. A dress of some sort. But when he, summoned by the egg timer, returned, she had turned around. And what a sight and what a shock. Large fat, milk-white breasts hanging and swaying around, behind a dress which was now pretty much undone. In a spongy mishmash of soap and water. In far too much soap and far too much water. The effect was nice though. Especially when she pretended not to notice it at all.

Christian didn't know what to do with himself. He turned off the cooker and poured cold water on the eggs.

And the pattern began to emerge. Evening after evening, whilst Christian was in the shower and more and more places, when he was on the stairs or using the kitchen.

But that was all it ever was. Even the evening when Ulla had waited for him like a failed caricature of a hooker. Waited for him in the living room doorway. Nothing actually happened.

It was too dark for them to be able to see properly. See each other. But he sensed her short, greasy hair. The thing he liked best about her.

Christian passed by holding his breath.

Ulla hissed.

He stopped. Frozen to the spot.

She moved towards him, but tripped on the step.

It wasn't funny.

Ulla ended up on the floor in the narrow hall. Had actually hurt herself quite badly. Christian just stood there with his prick stiffening behind the towel. Because, even though he found her ugly and unattractive it seemed to live its own life.

All the while, Ulla got to her feet shouting something. Not that she said anything in particular. She ran up the stairs. Disappeared and slammed the door.

After that episode nothing happened for a long time. Months. And then things, just fell into place in their own bizarre way. Ulla was secretly in love. Pushed letters of clumsy poetry under his door, but kept a reverential distance. Probably thought that the best thing was to go give it time. Probably thought that it was just a question *of* time. The poetry dried up though, after a while. But the thought was a good one. And they stayed on good terms and exchanged polite platitudes. Always with a glint of hope in her blue, blue eyes.

A fear that was both familiar and new now came in waves at the strangest times. Like the time when he stopped abruptly at the sight of an advert in the local supermarket. An advert for a course. It was all about building your confidence and physical strength at one and the same time. Weight training. It was a pointer, thought Christian. And soon he began both jogging and cycling.

Once in a while Christian went to a club with Mads and the noisy mates. But kept himself to himself. Couldn't comprehend the life he'd used to live. That he'd actually been a brash malcontent. Especially not now where he saw where Mads was today. No, he and his lot, they were just stupid. He'd rather stick to himself and his stubborn jottings.

He saw a young woman ride past on a bike as he stepped out into a suburban street. She dropped a letter. Christian stayed where he was. Felt that he'd seen it somewhere before. Deja-vu. He fixed his gaze on the letter. Wanted to pick it up, but didn't dare.

He hurried back to his room, where he ran out to the little balcony. Stood on tiptoes, but still couldn't see. Had to go back. Saw the wind take the letter and blow it up the street.

First when the letter was out of sight did he run towards it and pick it up. His heart thumping.

It was a message from an employer that a large sum of money would be transferred to a woman's account. A message which Christian suddenly felt he could turn to his advantage. He had achieved some sort of power. Felt important and big and significant. Felt that the whole world was his oyster. It had to be a sign. It *was* a sign.

The building had three stories. A large three-bedroom ground-floor flat with it's own private garden. A garden that smelt of elderberry.

The first time he went there no-one had been home, but the second time, a Sunday in May, he was in luck. The woman was in her late twenties. Tall and dark-haired. Friendly and happy. With a radiance that made him feel weak. Her natural ease and openness.

She'd sorted matters with a brief telephone call some time ago, and the letter which Christian thought she would be grateful to receive turned out to be worthless.

The woman invited him in and offered him coffee nonetheless, and wondered why he'd only contacted her now. Three days after the event.

The flat smelt of fresh-pressed garlic, and the rooms were warm and light. And Christian had never seen such a beautiful kitchen. So clean and proper. With a kitchen island and a hood and galvanised machines.

Espresso they called it. And a fruit presser. And a sieve and a food processor and kitchen knives. All neat and in good order. Although a couple of lazy kitchen cupboards were standing open. A couple of drawers that needed a shove and a couple of mugs and plates waiting to be washed up. But apart from that! Never so nice a home.

Christian adjusted himself to the circumstances. Now where there wasn't anything he could actually offer. Said he hadn't had time before.

Why hadn't he just called?

He shrugged his shoulders. Friendly. Wanted to be friendly. Felt intuitively that this was a good place to be. That he was comfortable and could breath and move easily and freely.

With Sarah. A woman full of a natural in-born positivity and satisfaction. A woman with a sense for colours and shapes. For the ability to let go and be yourself. For being a mother, for giving. Christian blushed at his thoughts without knowing why. Nonetheless that was what he felt.

She probably found him strange. Peculiar, thought Christian. With an undercurrent of danger, perhaps. It sounded good. Charmingly dangerous, yes. Or maybe she just thought him young. Awkward and clumsy? But cute, perhaps. Christian tried to think of something else, but couldn't let it go.

Was his posture too stooped? Did he clear his throat too often?

Even though Christian wanted to look cool, he found that he had great difficulty in controlling his body and his movements. And the damned sweat suddenly on his palms.

It was almost as if Sarah wanted to hold him, but shook off the thought. She stepped forward, but went no further, caught in two minds.

She looked at him. Said that just now she was very busy and would have to get on with things.

Christian nodded and answered yes, of course, but never got up. Asked her, instead, if she'd really read all those books on her shelves.

There were toys lying on the living room floor. A well-worn Danish poetry collection was open on the table. A DVD entitled 'A.T. & The Darkness' ...

Sarah smiled despite herself. Yes, she had. Some of them several times. Christian asked her where her children were.

Sarah answered that her son, Lucas, was spending a long weekend with his father.

Christian loved kids, he said. Really *loved* them. Had thought about becoming a teacher or working in a nursery.

Sarah took a quick look at the clock, as if she was thinking, maybe she'd give him another five minutes. Maybe she did have masses of things to do before her son, Lucas, came back and pulled the place apart again, thought Christian.

Sarah asked him whether he'd already finished high school, but seemed to regret her question almost as soon as she'd asked it.

Christian took no notice, but just said that he had, and that he was thinking of joining the army for a while before completing his education. He'd have to anyway. He'd already been drafted, and he might as well do it voluntarily.

Sarah asked him with more than a hint of surprise in her voice whether he'd considered the alternatives.

Yes, definitely. He hadn't really made up his mind yet. No the only thing he knew he wanted to be was a poet!

Then she was interested. Genuinely interested. Lived for Shelley and Shakespeare and Frost and Dickenson and Whitman and Wordsworth. And then there were all the Danes. Baidel and Strunge and Thomsen and Tafdrup, for example. It might be a bit old fashioned. And what about them? Christian nodded and said, well actually he preferred his own. Said that he'd lots of them at home and had already submitted several.

"Poetry collections?"

Sarah sounded surprised.

"Yeah, erm ... poetry collections."

"Who have you sent them to?"

And it was then that it just popped up. Just like that, of it's own accord. He could see everything, knew what course to follow.

"Them ... erm all of them. But-if-I-don't-become-a-poet-I-want-to-make-films."

"Films?"

"Yeah! Films. It's films I like best of all."

Christian looked down at the DVD on the floor.

They were quiet. There was surprise. Curiosity? A connection? Sarah seemed both confused and fascinated.

Christian asked Sarah whether she painted, and nodded at the walls on which a number of abstract paintings hung.

Sarah confirmed that she did and was met with a further question "But not portraits and stuff?"

She remained standing. Seemingly fascinated by his gaze. His eyes.

Fascinated by the way he sat. The way he spoke – the inflections that seemed so at variance with the fire in his eyes. So seemingly proper and correct, and yet with a sort of accumulated tension and something mournful in his eyes. Perhaps. She seemed, at any rate to take them in. The blue-grey eyes.

Their hands touched across the table, when she poured

more coffee.

Caught him looking at her breasts. Caught *her* biting her cheek. Maybe she was wondering how old he was? Sat talking to herself: Nineteen? Twenty? Twenty-one? Only to conclude that he seemed younger. He felt himself blush and rubbed his cheeks in an attempt to hide it, whilst he feverishly fumbled for new words.

Said, in a tone that to him sounded mature, that he thought she was good. That she had talent. Asked whether she would paint him. Shocked at his own suggestion – the implicit courage.

But, no, there was no way she could do that. It wasn't the sort of pictures she painted.

It seemed that she detected his disappointment, and because of it said that perhaps she could do a quick croquis, though there was something about her that said that she thought she was being stupid despite herself.

She sensed confusion and explained. A charcoal drawing. A drawing you do with a piece of charcoal.

Why charcoal? Why not just a pencil?

Well it was kind of ... Working in charcoal was just ... Sarah seemed caught up in her own enthusiasm. And began to explain and describe and touch. Touch with the greatest ease and naturalness.

She began to draw. And there was silence. As if it had been agreed. As of its own accord. With a feeling of tension. With a feeling of something naughty. Something forbidden. Of something one wanted to prevent but couldn't. An almost vibrating wall of humming accumulating energy. Of tension and of sultry sex.

He felt it. And he couldn't stop himself. *Wouldn't* stop himself. Found it right. Found it sexy and rude. Bloody rude.

He touched himself. Discretely but so that anyone who looked would see. Could feel that he was already on the point of overflowing.

First she was surprised. Then shocked, and began almost to laugh. Then afraid. Angry. Abused. Offended. Provoked. Elated. Lost. Bang. Totally and utterly overwhelmed. But decided, so it would seem, not to let herself be put out. Watched shamelessly.

He just sat. Looking at the floor.

"What are you doing? What the fuck do you think you're doing?"

He looked up. Unsure. Shifting from side to side. Had been mistaken. Very mistaken. Had to stop.

"I ... I just thought you'd like it."

She seemed to pull herself together and stood up. Walked back and forth and then stopped in front of him. Hit him hard in the face. Could see that it had already hurt. That he was already humiliated.

"Just go, please."

He could see from her expression that she felt sorry for him. Sorry for herself.

"I, I didn't mean to ... to upset you."

She seemed to sense his defeat.

Christian talked at the floor.

"I'm sorry. I … I shouldn't have done that of course. I just think that … that you're so hot."

She shook her head. Took him by the neck and pulled his head to her chest.

"Tush. Just sitting there with everything. You, you are a rude boy, aren't you?"

Sarah let him grope around and grab. Let him unfasten his trousers and pull up his shirt. Looked again at the clock and seemed to decide that there was still time before Lucas came home.

"Come. Lets go to the bed."

She whispered.

He followed obediently.

Sarah told him to relax. That there was plenty of time. That there was no rush.

She took him to her. Never seemed to feel him come. They fell apart.

She awoke and saw him sleeping. Curled up like a little bundle. Decided that somehow he looked like a child, despite his adult body.

A smile played across her lips. A smile that said that she liked him. Charming. Sweet. The smile disappeared and was replaced by a frown. She began to doubt herself. Was this all a big mistake? She let a finger move across his face. Carefully. Caringly. Then she let her hand rest on his body, relaxed and fell asleep.

Sarah didn't hear Lucas, before he was standing there

in the room asking "What are you doing?" and "Who's that, Sarah?"

It all seemed so wrong.

Lucas seemed to feel it instinctively and began to cry. Christian awoke while Sarah comforted her son.

Said that they liked each other, but that Christian was on his way out. Her ex had, as usual, just let Lucas run in up the garden on in his own.


Christian was in love. He thought he was in love. He *was* in love. Had found a purpose in life. Had begun to believe in himself. Had found Sarah, he thought, and began almost to cry.

Christian began to keep a diary. And wrote poetry. Especially poetry. About love and sex, about closeness and beauty and sunshine and warmth. And everything just went his way. Came in an unending mingling. And he *was* a poet.

He wrote for hours and hours. He wrote and he wrote and he wrote. Preferably in rhyme and rhythmic verse, but also in more daring prose poems, which he hadn't really liked, at least not at first.

Borrowed barrow loads of poetry books. Ploughed through them all. And cried and laughed and saw that he was not alone. That there were people who thought as he did. Felt as he did.

But he was better. Had to be better. He just knew it. Completely forgot all about films.

He filled her letterbox with declarations of love. Stood

and waited outside her workplace till she came out. Followed her at a distance and discovered that she picked up Lucas from Gran and Grandad's after they'd picked him up from kindergarten.

Learnt, that Sarah liked to do her shopping from real shops run by shopkeepers, not the supermarket, that she cycled almost everywhere, and that she loved her child more than anything else.

She worked four days a week, and on her day off Lucas was almost never in kindergarten. Then they'd go out together and visit Gran and Grandad. In a house a couple of streets down from Christian's.

The weekends were spent working in the little kitchen garden in front of the flat and visiting her family. A big family. A nice family. Her one and all, after Lucas of course. Cousins and brothers and sisters. Who were all happy and all asked after each other, and they kissed and hugged so much that Christian – when he actually, later on, was introduced to them – thought that they must all suffer from some terrible sex deficit, what with all that touching.

The second time they met, after weeks of following her, after weeks of Christian pulling himself together, Sarah had evidently planned ahead and taken precautions.

After a long period of ambivalence and long conversations with her friend Sine she'd decided to see Christian, to give him a chance, and to see what came of it. Not that she had much hope. Not at all, there was just something about him, as she explained to her friend.

And Sine had supported her and backed her up. Had of course could understand the problem, but knew her friend well enough to see that she was already in love. Very in love so it would seem. Otherwise she wouldn't have spent all that time talking and thinking about him.

And what if he was young? It wasn't a huge difference. Eight, nine years? She should feel flattered, said the friend and laughed.

He was so sensitive, laughed Sarah ironically. Evidently aware that there was some truth in what she said. And so attentive. Very different to the other men she'd known. And it wasn't as if Lucas was getting a new dad ... he was Sarah's boyfriend that was all. That was her mantra. She didn't want to be alone, and that it was really nice having a man about the place. Was there supposed to be just one true form of love? How love should come about? No, surely not. And love makes us blind.

Friend Sine had just nodded and listened.

Or was it a question of pity? Maternal instincts and protectiveness? Maybe. She left it at that. At any rate she was willing to find out. And that meant giving Christian a chance, a proper chance. She didn't want him to suffer for her capriciousness. Sine agreed and Sarah was happy.

And in time the doubts receded. And the questions

were forgotten. Just like so many other things in life.

And Christian was fired up like never before. So happy and so easy and so glad. Became Lucas' best friend. Fooled around and mucked about and played. Learnt to hug. Learnt that a kiss was more than just sex. Learnt to express himself and to have an opinion. To discuss and debate. That one could disagree without becoming enemies and fighting. That books weren't all forced on one. That art was more than just baying stags and flying ducks. That food could be made, eaten and enjoyed. That wine was a vintage and gin was a drink. That pot was for smoking and clothes for wearing with style.

And Christian grew with it. Avoided military service. Got friends and other habits. Began to believe in a future and started working with children in the same institution as Sarah.

With the money from his cleaning job, his income started to exceed his expenses quite significantly, and Christian started seeing films. Lots of films. But the past was a closed book. They never talked about it. His past. The past that crept up on him anyway. With twisted thoughts and peculiar tendencies. Like when she asked about his parents and his older brother. And he had a sister too, didn't he?

Yeeahh, Christian didn't remember saying that.

But his mother, what about his mother? Yes, she was good. Not that they saw much of each other. She was busy.

Perhaps they should visit her?

No, she didn't like meeting new people. Had told him that she didn't want any visitors. And, of course she had her boyfriend.

But Christian visited her. Alone. And always came back full of praise for some new film that Sarah just had to see.

Hadn't he been to see his mum?

Yes, yes. It was just something he'd heard from a colleague.

Perhaps they should go and see the film together?

Sure. When he had the time. He was busy right now. With books about films and the latest film news.

And what about his brother? His brother? ... ... Well, yeah, his brother.

And time passed. And with time came time for schools and lessons. A time where he dropped his job in the kindergarten. And with time came knowledge and high school exams. And the still more frequent recurring questions. From Sarah, who absolutely couldn't stop herself from prying. Wanted to know. Where did he come from? And why did he never talk about himself? About his childhood. And if there was something he was sitting on, it was going to affect him for the rest of his life.

But Christian shut her out. Simply couldn't cope with her. With all her nonsense and her talk of psychoanalysis and psychotherapy and psycho-this-that-and-the-other-bullshit. It made him feel sick.

What the fuck did she take him for? She was the psychopath with all her ridiculous questions. Couldn't she just leave him in peace?

But she could see it. That he was struggling. That there was something weighing on him, holding him back.

Shit, fuck, arse, cunt. That was what it was. Even though the terms in the psychology books burned in his stomach, he was not going to think about it. Never. Even though he couldn't run away from the doubt. The lurking doubt as to whether anything was worth it.

And with a strange indolence when things were at their very worst. And the thought, the thought that, actually, he didn't need to study at all. That he actually was familiar with most of it already. That none of it really mattered, when it came down to it. The periods during which Christian could just barely creep through a day and an evening at the school. When books once more meant compulsion and unpleasant discipline.

And why now? And where did it all come from? Everything had been going so well. His cough came back. His banging the open doors. They *had* to be shut. Couldn't they understand, for fuck's sake?! She just mixed everything up. And Lucas was allowed to get away with almost anything, he made even more of a mess. Didn't they know anything about tidiness? And where was she when she was round at Sine's? Was she round at Sine's? What about the evening when he'd called her? The evening when she wasn't there?

She'd just mispronounced it. Got the words jumbled

up. Misspoken. That was all. She'd been round at Stine's. And why she'd said Sine, well she'd no idea. Stine, Sine. Sine, Stine. It happened. Anybody could make that kind of slip.

But it was that evening when she'd not felt like sex. There were the other evenings when she'd not felt like sex.

Absolutely. Exactly. That was it.

Did he really think that she was seeing someone else.

"Mmn, maybe, how should I know?"

"I wouldn't be able to live with myself."

Christian shrugged his shoulders.

"Even though I'm not good enough in bed?"

"Do we really have to talk about that all the time? It's getting too much for me."

"Or was that just you misspeaking again?"

"Christian – look, just stop it okay. And, anyway, I didn't say that you weren't good enough in bed. You asked me what I wanted and I answered."

"Well, wasn't I right?!"

Sarah sighed. This was all getting a bit too much.

"It doesn't matter that much, and there are other ways of doing it, and I think it's fine. I think it's fine, the way it is. It doesn't matter much."

"But you want it anyway don't you? Want me to lick you."

"Oh, for fuck's sake!"

"But I'm right, aren't I?!"

Now she just sounded tired.

"Yeah, sure Christian, you're right."

"And what can we do about that?"

Sarah decided apparently, not to go on. Not to let things get to the pitch that they had so many times before. That would be too futile. A waste of time. A waste of energy. She seemed, at any rate, to want to change course and alter her tactics. To the ones that worked, that she knew would work.

"Can't we just drop it now? Eh?"

She moved towards him and up against him.

"It means a lot for a bloke to know that his girlfriend is satisfied."

"It's okay Christian. You're still my man."

He didn't answer. Instead he put his hand on her breasts. Then he took a good handful and massaged them. Undid her blouse and let them flop out.

Right in his face.

He massaged and lifted and kissed and squeezed and pressed. These breasts. These so delightful breasts. Fantastic attributes. A woman's most prominent feature. An object of constant interest and unending fascination. These great pomegranates – preferably really big ones. These swollen, swinging, swaying, dangling, hopping , jumping, lifted ... melons. Tits, knockers, headlights, jubblies, honkers, assets, hooters, jugs, boobs, breasts. She stiffened. It hurt. They were sore. It was actually a bit unpleasant. Would have liked to pull away, but didn't. Was familiar with the routine and the procedure and began to undo her trousers. Seemed to know what would happen, just like Amen in church.

The power of habit, its force. Small nightly routines. The daily grind. Sarah didn't understand his reluctance. Now, when he was almost finished. Why just give up? Why not go the whole way and finish off properly? If he wanted to go on to further study, like he'd said. Why wasn't he revising? Why just sit there and see TV? And why did he suddenly go out and not come back till morning? Why did he never say anything about himself? Why had she never seen his mother? And why did he watch all those sick-making documentaries about mass murderers and Nazi Germany? That is, when he wasn't just playing computer games?
Why was he always going on about other people's successes? Never his own? It was always celebrities. Made as big a deal as possible. Like Bille August travelling to the US, and showing Isabel Allende *'Pelle The Conqueror* - Pelle Erobreren' after which they let him make *'The House of Spirits* - Aandernes Hus,' for example.
And why had he stopped writing poetry? And why didn't he make films instead. Apply to the film school? Because Christian was bound to be just as good as all the others.
He didn't have to compare himself all the time to people he had nothing in common with. He just had to believe in himself and get on with it. Then things would

turn out all right. *She* believed in him. But she couldn't do it on her own.

He was so kind and loving to Lucas – why not make a children's film, for example? A short film?

Actually the thought had already crossed his mind. Just not right now. First he needed inspiration. Hitler and Mussolini and goose stepping and parades. Flapping flags and blustering banners and the ongoing fascination. The need to feel the titillating tingling and the hairs that stood to attention on his arms and neck. Which rose in time with the bark of '*Heil*' from thousands of throats. Just needed to feel the heat and the enthusiasm one more time.

Of course it was all wrong, what they stood for. But they had style, you couldn't get away from that. Style and discipline and everything in its proper place. '*Ordnung muss sein*'.

Not like motorcycle gangs and their amateurish biker badges. When they came rumbling past in a noisy cavalcade. They were just pathetic. Of course they were. A bunch of wimps when it came down to it.

Or like the really wealthy. In the open-top sports cars or the big Mercedes and Jaguars. They were just braggarts and their dicks were tiny.

Or like the beat of Wagner and hiphop and rap and thudding subwoofers, when the really absurd ridiculous twats came cruising past in their pimped rust buckets. With their windows rolled down and their hair gelled back shouting at anything that so much as smelt of a woman.

Or when the police came shooting past, sirens blazing. Twats the lot of them and bumpkins.

And then there was studying. Having a university degree was a good thing they said.

No, he'd be better off making films. That was what he really wanted to do, wasn't it? If only he didn't have all that doubt. The nagging, enervating doubt which popped up at the most inconvenient times.

And, if it was to be film, what should he go for? It would have to be directing. But he hadn't much experience now, had he?

Perhaps he should rent a camera? Or just drop in on a production company?

Thomas Klerke ... Sarah had found a phone number in Christian's wallet.


The sun broke out over London. It was morning. Christian was drunk like never before. He had to vomit. Stumbled out to the bathroom, kneeling in front of the toilet bowl.

Natasha woke surprised and tried to get an explanation out of him. But Christian just wanted to sleep. Natasha got up and spent the time on herself before they had to check out of the hotel. He was still drunk when she woke him.

# 8

Christian and Natasha moved in together.

Natasha studied, whilst Christian worked as a video or production assistant. He had a new idea inside him, in his head and his gut. A film about growing up. A film, about taking responsibility.

He wrote, and he fought with his shame and applied once more for money from everywhere he could think of. He talked and told and did what he could, and again, but it made no difference. It seemed as if no-one was listening.

In the end he just gave up and went round with a chip on his shoulder and complained. Felt, that it was all just a load of shit, and that there was no hope in it, that everyone was against him and all they wanted to do was hold him back, whilst Natasha just shut herself in and revised for her exams. Wondered perhaps at the start that he never asked after her, just took her for granted – expected her to be ready for sex when he wanted it. Was upset. Felt hurt and used. Said that nothing she did seemed to matter to him. He'd studied too, hadn't he? He ought to know that it was sometimes hard. And why did he never help her? And why did he always try to change the subject when she wanted to talk institution analysis, media theory, film history or intermedial expressions, for example? And why did Christian always smile like that and say that it was a long time since he'd studied anything, and that, perhaps, he forgot things quicker than most? And why did he always say that was just what made them different?

But gradually, Natasha just shut herself more and more off and eventually seemed to not to let it affect her any more. Seemed to have found her own inner rhythm and just let Christian be Christian. Thought that it was okay. Actually quite liked the fact that he didn't get involved in her affairs all the time. That he gave her space to find her own answers. Wasn't like her other boyfriends who were always tearing about being clever on her behalf.

One thing though she couldn't let go. One thing that was just too much. His continuous complaining and his stubborn and eternal rants about Steven Spielberg the craftsman, Quentin Tarantino the idiot and that amateur Steven Soderbergh.

Finally Natasha was almost ready to flip and felt compelled to try and do something, for both their sakes. She still loved him, didn't she? He was still Christian. Or had he changed? Had she? Or were they just growing apart, as they called it.

Even though it was a commonplace, a cliché, a banal and stupid phrase, just one of those things people said, she still struggled frequently with the thought. She still loved him. But knew him better, as she said.

Natasha seemed to take a decision. What if Christian travelled to the States? Natasha knew someone studying English who'd probably be more than happy to earn a bit on the side and translate one of his scripts. Yeah, and then he could get his brother to set up a couple of meetings. He must know lots of producers and agents and directors. And then she could stay home and study all the while.

Christian considered it. For a long time. Of course he'd thought of getting a couple of his scripts translated, he said, he just hadn't got round to it. But the idea was a good one. And the brother thing. He'd thought of that too, actually. But was it really for the best? And what about Natasha and him?

Christian felt suddenly scared. Uncertain of their future together. Uncertain of his own future. Because he loved her. He knew that now. And he didn't want to lose her – rather anything than that.

It would work out, said Natasha. They could trust each other. And he didn't have to stay there for his whole life did he? Christian was still hesitant. Wanted Natasha to accompany him.

But she couldn't afford it, and anyway there were her studies to think of.

But she could finish them at *USC* – University of Southern California – or *UCLA*.

Yes, but only in two terms' time, and at a price she couldn't afford - didn't have a hope of paying.

But even with all this well-meant advice Christian never got any further with things. Only with his work, where there was plenty to do. So much, in fact, that he hadn't the energy to do anything other than watch telly. Stuff about a couple of teenagers from Colorado who went amok one day and killed thirteen people, for example. And he never saw his friends. And the café might as well be in ruins for all he knew. He didn't go there any more. Not now there were two of them in the flat. Now there were two of them in the flat and Natasha started to feel that it was a bit too small. Started getting some sort of claustrophobic attacks – even though she appeared to want the best – she just had to get out. Couldn't *take* it. Started asking more and more insinuating questions about Christian. About Christian's brother.

Why did he always put the phone down as soon as she stepped into the room? Did she embarrass him? Had he told anybody that she even existed? And why was it always Christian, that called the brother and not the other way round?

Christian answered – as always – that the brother was a busy man who spent a lot of time working in England or the Czech Republic or Spain or Italy or wherever. They made a lot of commercials down there actually. And it was just more convenient that it was Christian who called his brother and not the other way round.

But he never came to Denmark?

Never to Denmark, no. No-one had heard of him in Denmark, no-one at all. He'd managed to keep a low profile when it came to Denmark.

But didn't USA have everything? All the climates you could want? All the equipment? Why work in Europe?

It must be expensive.

Expensive?! No, far from it. It was actually much, much cheaper. Both in terms of studio space and film crews and equipment. That's why they did it. To save money. Because she was right, otherwise there'd be no reason to travel all the way to Europe. And then again, when he refused to make films with Natasha – just bypass the system and with himself as the producer as she'd suggested – when he wouldn't even let her read his stuff, why not just do things properly? Try and get someone in Hollywood to take a look at them? Hadn't she given him Ann's number ages ago? What was holding him back? Natasha was just getting so bloody tired of him always complaining and never doing a thing about it. Was so bloody tired of her ideas never being good enough for him.

And Christian smoothed things over and was kind and understanding. Because he loved her. He loved her really.

Natasha started going out in the evenings, sometimes several in a row, whilst Christian just stayed home watching TV. Watched programme after programme about highly fascinating killings and mass murderers. Couldn't really get his act together to do anything. Seemed to be waiting for something. Seemed to need to recharge, or just pull himself together. But couldn't. Didn't want to. Did, in the end, get it together to call Ann and came home proud and happy with his translated script. And Natasha was happy again. Proud. There was only one thing lacking now. Because there was no point in just leaving it to rot in a drawer, was there?

And Christian felt cornered and turned aggressive. Didn't talk sense. But Natasha kept at it. Here was Christian with a great opportunity. He had a good script, as he said, in English, he had a connection and he had money. So what was he waiting for? Or did she have to book the flight for him too?

Yeah, well then he'd start by going to New York.

New York?! What about Hollywood?

Yeah, yeah. But there were production companies on the east coast as well. And that was where the brother spent most of his time -when he wasn't actually in Hollywood. Maybe he'd get lucky and run into him. Just like that.

Wouldn't it be a good idea if Christian called him first?

No, no, best to let it be a surprise. No, she should let him do things his way. In any case he knew more about the system.

In the States?

Christian chose to ignore this question and just enjoyed the feeling of renewed enthusiasm. Fresh optimism, a reborn hope. Not just in himself, but in Natasha too. Natasha who shone like a sun from a cloud-free sky. Who said that she was pregnant. Just like that, in the middle of everything.

But he never left. Couldn't get it together to go. Didn't really have the money, so he said. And he couldn't travel now, not when she was expecting.

Natasha felt stuck in rut. The sparkle disappeared from her eyes. Turned cold.

"I think that what you've told me about your brother is just a pack of lies, Christian. And if you lie to me again I'm going to leave you."


"Thank-you! Super, great! Really, really good. We're really getting there now. One more time, please."

"Sound!"

"Speed."

"Camera?!"

"... rolling!"

"117, take nine!"

*Smack!*

"Set!"

"Aaaaaand action!"


Sarah confronted him with her telephone conversation with Thomas. Crying and angry. She wanted an explanation. He never tried to defend himself. Not until after he'd moved out.

It was all just lies. Lies all of it. All of it. Couldn't she see that? No, he supposed she couldn't. It must be hard to understand when you were just a normal everyday person. When you didn't have to be constantly on your guard, looking out for paparazzi and unscrupulous sensationalist journalists. Because that was how it was. That was why.

Christian had the story ready. Ready just in case they ever met. By chance. He missed her. Missed Lucas.

He lay there, staring up at the dirty ceiling in his expensive room. The paint was peeling and discoloured.

The room was cold. He didn't want to turn on the heating. Was past caring.

It was just an emergency lie. For use in a situation where things got out of hand. So what if the brother lived in Denmark, was human and perfectly ordinary. Couldn't she see that that was how it all fitted together? That when you were successful you had to protect yourself for the sake of privacy. So you could live. So you could survive. Christian thought of calling her. Or just dropping by. But gave it up. No, it was time to move on. Onwards, upwards. And as fast as possible.

What the hell was she doing anyway? Going through his pockets and then *calling* his brother.

She was all-right, wasn't she? So well-informed, so clever. So tolerant, no prejudices. And that Lucas was just a little spoilt brat. Suddenly he hated her. Hated her for everything she was and did and stood for. What the fuck had he seen in her anyway? She hadn't even been very good in bed. And how many women hadn't he had on the side? Three? Four? More? Clara from work. He'd just pulled her out into the toilet on a lunch break.

Stine, Sarah's friend. Or was it Sine?

Karen, definitely. From the German evening class. And a few here and there he'd picked up at the café. He'd had them all. And they loved it. Whores the lot of them. Every one.

Not for money maybe, no preferably something a little more sophisticated. A bit more subtle and indirect. But there was a payment involved. No question. Nothing was free in this life. And no-one would just give for the sake of giving. Everyone wanted something in return. Prestige, a better job, something to gossip about. And of course the money. Just with the predicate of girlfriend or wife. Which gave them something to hide behind. Anything direct would just be too vulgar, of course. But where was the love? The real love. The love that was for giving without a thought of getting something in return. Was there such a thing? Or was it just all a load of drivel, based on the usual light-touch with the Bible?

All you had to do was give. Give of yourself. And was there room for that? Time for that? A reason for it? When everything just came down to money at the end of the day. Cold, loveless money. But Christian could give. He had lots to give. He just needed to start.


"And thank-you! ... One more time, please! Keep the feeling – don't let it go!"

"Final checks, please ... ... All right, thank you ... Sound!"
"Speed."
"Camera!"
"... rolling!"
"117, take ten!"
*Smack!*
"Set!"
"Action!"


"Well, what is there to say? There's nothing to say."
"There's plenty. Do you have a brother at all?"
"... ..."
"Why can't you tell me?"
"I've got to go to work now Natasha. I'm going to have to go. I love you. I really love you."
He went to kiss her, and she turned her cheek to him.

The day turned into a real nightmare. Christian had messed things up. Argued with most of them. And the feeling had spread. Wormed its way into even the smallest crevices. Out to the production room where the producer suddenly couldn't get things to work. And it all ended up back on Christian's plate again.
Just as the crew were on their way home, Christian was called to one side and told that they weren't going to need him tomorrow anyway. The production manager was sorry, but they just didn't have enough money to

hire him for two days – the budget wouldn't stretch to it. This was unusual, and Christian was smart enough to put two and two together. His arguments with the others had got too much, and someone had complained. Was it the grip? Little jerk. Or the best boy. He was a real spastic.

The production manager stopped him in mid flow. No, actually it had been the customer. The customer. And the customer was always right.

Okay, well Christian wanted to stick around anyway just to put his tapes in order. So he could hand over a reasonable product at least. The production manager shrugged his shoulders and went home, without saying goodbye.

The others were long gone. And since they'd be working again tomorrow the only thing they'd taken down was the camera. And they'd taken away the film. The raw stock and the exposed material which was already on its way to the lab. Everything else was just left so it was ready for the next day's shooting.

Christian finished tidying his notes and rewound the last video tape. The machine had malfunctioned, and they'd had to replace it with another one. And they'd lost the time code. It was this that had led to the day's first argument between Christian and the first assistant cameraman.

The stage manager had asked Christian to tell him when he'd finished so that he could lock up for the night, and had gone off to his car that was parked on the other set. A set that wasn't being used at the minute. Some part or other had evidently fallen of the car's undercarriage, and, of course, it was handy that you could just park your car in one of the empty studios and use it as a workshop.

Christian got up and walked over to the door. Strangely his head was completely clear. Crystal clear actually.

He turned round to study the set. The heavy lamps, that made noises as they cooled, the lamp stands which were just as heavy, the flags and the so-called cutters used for creating the perfect light and the perfect shadows, the cables, the dolly, the rails, the crane, the set and the props. The walls decked with glass wool sound insulation, the lines across the ceiling. The ladders. The coffee table with the half-empty thermoses, the sweets and the warm cookies. The chairs for the customer, the bureau and the director. And their monitor. Christian's own table at the back of the room.

He started from one end of the room and worked his way through it. Never found out quite how far he'd got. Not before he heard loud shouts and curses and felt a heavy hand on his shoulders. And that was, of course, too late. Far too late. Several of the lamps were already broken, most of the set was smashed. Props were strewn everywhere and broken into thousands of tiny pieces. Everything was chaos. But Christian still felt completely empty inside.

The stage manager stood and shouted himself hoarse,

about how much Christian was going to pay and how he would, never, ever get to work in the film industry again. He was going to call the police, but decided to call the production manager first, and ten minutes later he came running. By then Christian was on his way out. The stage manager stood in his way and held him back, until the production manager could come over the shock, and a couple of minutes later a young policeman turned up with a note block, whilst his colleague wandered round inspecting the set. Then they let him go.


"Cut! Last time."
"Sound!"
"Speed."
"Camera!"
"... rolling!"
"117, take eleven!"
*Smack!*
"Set!"
"Action!"


Christian woke up with a headache. He rolled onto his side and fell asleep again.
Later, much later he found himself sitting on the floor in the middle of the living room. In a home that was home no longer, definitely not now that Natasha had

moved in with her parents, but just a place with roof and walls and naked furniture. Christian drank and drank. Drank himself completely senseless. He fell around between the living room, the bedroom and the kitchen and only went out when he needed something to drink. He didn't have the appetite for anything else. He dug out one of his moving boxes and began throwing scripts out. Threw everything out. Without looking at them. Without thinking. Without reflecting. Without so much as a glance at a single page. He sung and hummed at the same time. Mumbled to himself. Then he pulled the box bump bump down the back stairs and out into the yard, where he stood and pissed on it. Then he thought better of it. Put his hand down into the soggy contents, fished out a sheet of paper that was more or less dry and set fire to it. A minute later the entire box and its contents were in flames.

One day took another. The living room was dark. The room was dark. Things started to smell. To stink. He stank. Had thrown up in the sink several times and pissed all over the toilet. Had left the fridge open. Had let food be food and only let bottles collect. Bottles and paper. Handwritten notes that just flew out onto the floor in front of him at the pace of his bodily fluids.

Then it was over. The day when somebody or other came and knocked on his door.

Christian just opened the door and stood there glowering.

"I have to know this."

The woman remained standing on the stairs. Standing there holding the hand of a little silent boy with big eyes.

Christian didn't recognise her.

"What? Who the fuck are you?"

"Tina. Thomas' wife."

Christian tried to focus.

"And what is it?"

"Is this true?"

Tina shoved a cheap manilla folder at him.

"What is it?"

"Articles. About his ... feats."

"What do you want me to do about it?"

"So it's true?"

"What are you talking about?"

Christian took in the contents of the folder. Brief paragraphs with unpleasant headings.

"You ought to speak to him. Even though ... he talks about you a lot."

"I don't know him."

Tina didn't answer, just whispered a couple of words to the boy to hurry him along. Seconds later they were on their way down the stairs again.

Christian stumbled out onto the stairs and stuck his head between the railings.

"I don't fucking know him, all-right!!"

# 9

It was a tiny room. The walls were grey-white and covered in faded graffiti. A table and two chairs.
Christian sat silently waiting. Then the sound of steps came from the long corridor, and he knew it was him.
The prison officer opened the door and stepped to one side so Thomas could come in.
He seemed bigger, taller than Christian remembered.
"I almost refused to come. You know that, don't you?"
Christian shrugged his shoulders and stood up.
They stood in silence.
The guard closed the door behind them, and left them to themselves.
"I just wanted to see how you were doing."
"You fucking little shit, man. Get the fuck out of here, or I'll fucking have you. Three years in this hole and you turn up now?! What are you playing at, for fuck's sake?"
"I haven't come to apologise."
"I don't want any fucking apologies, all right. Do you know who I am? I'm the fucking king. The king of kings. The best, the biggest and the fucking strongest. But I have to fight anyway. Fight all the time with those pathetic little arseholes. And for what?! Why can't people just take a chill and leave me alone? You too? I hate people. Get that? Especially the fat, the ugly and the fucking stupid ... Are you fucking stupid Christian,

are you? Eh?"

"Look, let's sit down, eh?"

Christian sat down.

"And all their fucking therapists, man. They just want to poke and rummage and fuck with your head. They make you think. And that's not what I do most. Is it, eh? No Christian, me, I like to do things. Action. I do what I'm good at. If you think too much, you burn out. So much that you can't move any more."

Thomas nodded to Christian.

"Look at yourself, man. You're solid like a fucking rock ... Look, pop by my flat, will ya? Just to see if everything's okay? They can get up to all sorts of tricks, the bastards."

"Sit down, won't you?"

Thomas wrenched out a chair and sat on it deliberately.

"Fuck man, I've really missed you. What the fuck are you doing with yourself? You could have popped by, you know. Just once in a while. I mean, I'm not going anywhere am I?"

"It's been difficult. I've been busy."

"Don't get me wrong little brother. I'm just proud of you man."

"There's nothing I've done you should be proud of Thomas"

"Shut the fuck up. Who's the one in the nick? It's like I say. You're the smart one, right? You got on with your life. But you could go visit your mum every now and then."

"We live as best we can, don't we? You live your life. I live mine."

"What about Tina? And Arnold? You haven't seen them have you? I need to fucking get out of here. Otherwise the crafty cow will run off to the other side of the moon. And who'd help her then, eh? And a couple of days out every now and then is just not fucking enough. Maybe I should just get myself a *ho*. On the side you know. A little Thai bitch you can just stick your cock in whenever you want to. But then I'd have to look out for her. And I haven't got the money. Anyway it's for losers running around with a Thai *ho*. Fuck that, I say. I don't care, I just need some pussy ... Can you get me some pussy, Christian? Oh, what the fuck, I just need to get away. They can't manage on their own, not Arnold anyway ... couldn't you just stick your head round the door, see if they're okay?"

Christian shrugged his shoulders and wondered where Thomas got all that energy from. His apparently unstoppable stream of speech.

"Okay, sure. I can do that."

"Yeah, it's mostly just to keep a bit of an eye on Arnold. I don't know if I trust the little mare any more. She's a real bitch, you know ... I need to start training again. Quit the fags and the bad vibes. Clean cut. Straight from the top. No more fucking about. Every day. Weight training, you know so that I can get into shape properly. You just have to plan it right. Do you work out? I wouldn't fucking do it in here you know. Fucking faggots. What's wrong with *the hotbox*, anyway? It's just the others that are a bunch of *shit splitters*. Solitary is nothing man. It's cool. Gets you away from all the fuckwits …

The only problem is money. I've only got ten big ones left. But as soon as I'm out again, I'll just push a few *blanks*. And I can always just call Johan. He's cool … Like the other times, you know. Just borrow 60K and then you're rolling. A hire car to pick up the goods, stuff it in the tires, drive back, and you're home and dry. The fucking pigs are too stupid to notice. It takes a crook to kill a crook …

Yeah well, fuck that. As long as they let me be. Except for the *towel heads*. Why the fuck do they never go out alone?! Fucking wusses … If you met them on their own they'd shit themselves. Then I'd do 'em over one at a time, cut them into bits and feed them to some pigs … That'd be fucking funny … A pigsty?!"

Christian tried to smile, but it didn't really work.

"Even the fucking gym has started to stink of fucking *Paki* sweat. That's actually why I don't go there any more. Only when I'm selling *smack*. What you need is a little gym at home. Do you work out?"

"Every now and then. Can't you just ask your social worker?"

"Fuck off, will you. Of course I fucking can't. She'll just ask me all those pathetic questions. Just like at the mental health test with that bloody psycholotrist or whatever the fuck he was."

"The psychiatrist."

"That's what I fucking said wasn't it? He said I was a psychopath. Which is fine by me. It's like what I say. I'm the fucking king. Not like the other dickwads. Apart from that he was just a faggot. Just like all the others. They're too easy man ... Anyway, it's none of her fucking business what I do. I mean, is it her money? Fuck off is it. She can just fuck off and shut the fuck up, the stupid cow. Maybe I should just give her a good seeing to, eh? Pass her up in an alley, and then just shove my great fat prick up her arse. You know what? I think the little mare would like that. She's too ugly, though.

No, they can come and 'ave some. All of them. Fucking retards. I'll give 'em a good kicking. I haven't done shit. No more than others would. Not a fucking thing. The fucking arseholes. And all the *towel heads* are fucking queens all of them. They all fuck each other up the arse. Sick mothers. And then there's all their shit brown *hos* – they need a good seeing to. One at a time. Fuck and chuck 'em about."

Finally, Christian broke in through the solid wall of words and constant flow of speech.

"I wanted to talk to you about ... about Dad. About us. So I could kind of get to know you perhaps."

"What the fuck are you on about?! You know me well enough. You're my kid brother, aren't you?"

"Yeah, but, I mean ... there's so much ... I can't really

remember any more."

"Look, shutting things out. That's just normal. Who the fuck doesn't do that? I do that all the time. Then I just take some coke, smash up a *Paki*, and I'm back on top again."

"Do you remember what happened? I mean everything when we were kids?"

"Of course. But that's all in the past now, isn't it. I mean, you get on with your fucking life."

"I just want to know, who you are. And why the fuck you reacted the way you did. Really. Seriously."

"Are you off your head?! What the fuck are you playing at? Drop all that psychobabble piss for fuck's sake."

"No, no, no, no. Look, it's got fuck all to do with psychology. It's just me, I want to know! I need to know stuff, so I can get on with my life. Come on man."

"Aww, poor little brother, eh? I bet you have a real hard life, whilst the rest of us are just rotting away in the nick. You always were a fucking little spoilt brat."

"Can't you just tell me about yourself Thomas? And just leave me out of it, okay? That's all I'm asking."

"What do you want to know?"

"Just stuff. You know!"

"Stuff?"

"Yeah stuff, for fuck's sake. Anything."

"Don't play the wise guy Christian, or I'll fucking have you. And it won't make any difference that we're brothers."

"I'm not being a wise guy Thomas. For the first time in

my life, I'm not. Look, will you tell me, or won't you?"
Thomas leant back in his chair. Looked at Christian in an overweening way.

"Stuff ... I like stuff. If that's what you want to know. I'm really fond of my new microwave, for example. It's got more watts than the old one. I bought it the last time I was out on release. Tina was very pleased with it. And of course there's the TV and the DVD player. And I've got a new mobile ... Tina's got that right now but ... And the computer, of course. Not that I play much ... But I might want to if there was a porn game or something. That would be really funny ... But I mean otherwise we just live like people normally do, even though ... can you get me a new flat do you think? I mean don't you know a load of, or ... I mean it's okay the one we've got. And we look after it. It's in good nick. There are just so many fucking *towel heads* round there."

Christian shook his head.

"What else? I mean what else do you do?"

"Other stuff? Well, there's my magazines ... body building and martial arts, right? It's a while since I did any karate. I bet you didn't know that, eh little brother?"

"That sounds cool."

"I mean I used to, not at the minute."

"Are you good at it then? I mean black belt and stuff?"

"Yeah, yeah, I mean ... not exactly. I got an injury and

then I had to stop, you know how it is."

"Okay ... You read a lot of magazines. What about books?"

"Yeah, yeah comic books. Every now and then. Otherwise it's Science Illustrated maybe, that sort of stuff. I think that's pretty cool. And magazines about computer games of course."

"...?"

"...!"

"And ...?"

"Body building and the solarium every once in a while. That's pretty cool. I used to really like cars, but that didn't last. It's too fucking expensive to really style a car properly. And then there's the blokes who ride around in that sort of thing. Real losers arseholes, you know ..."

"What about mates? I mean, have you got lots of friends?"

"No, not really. Not my scene. I used to hang out with one of Tina's friends, but it all got a bit much."

"I mean that's the way things normally work, isn't it?"

"Yeah, that's not the way we do things here little brother – that's more for faggots. I don't need friends anyway. I can handle myself. I'm used to it. But business, that's different. I have people to help me with stuff."

"What do you really think about Mum and Dad and our upbringing? "

"Upbringing?! What sort of word is that? You were there too, you little fuck."

"Not all the time. And you've been through things I haven't. Can't you just tell it like you remember it?"

"From the beginning you mean?"

"Just something. Just start."

"I don't know … At the start I thought it was difficult. And this is just between you and me, all-right?!"

Christian nodded.

"If this gets out you're dead, all-right?!"

"Yeah, come on, just get on with it. Who would I tell it to anyway?"

"You are *so* close to the line Christian."

"What are you afraid of?"

"Look, it's nobody else's business where I come from, okay!"

"You're not the only one with a load of shit to deal with you know."

Thomas broke out into unexpected laughter.

"You're a cocky little shit all of a sudden. You didn't used to be like that … where the fuck did that come from? That confidence? You didn't get that from your 'upbringing.' It's not like it just happens is it? I mean, it wasn't something I used to have either. You should have seen my fingers man. I used to bite them something awful."

"You mean your nails. I know how it is."

"And they bled all the time. Because, of course, I couldn't stop myself from biting the skin off as well. But you wouldn't remember that. It was before your time."

Thomas paused for a second. Then he continued:

"Oh yeah, and I had these spasms. Do you remember that? I must've looked like a spastic. I just couldn't help myself. With the nose and arms and legs, you know. It was like I had to make sure that I could stretch properly all the time.

I had those for a long time – years. You remember that don't you? Especially all that with my nose. I just had to pull my upper lip down over my teeth, you know, so that my mouth and nose got straightened right out. It was kind of calming. I tried to stop myself, but it was like I was about to explode. It's all-right now of course, but back then. Fuck, man."

"What about what happened at home. How did you see that?"

"That was okay ... I don't have any problems with that."

"Of course it wasn't fucking okay. A little two room flat. And me and Birgitte who had to share 'till she moved out. That was pretty fucking far from okay. And Mum and Dad ..."

"Yeah and Mum who slept in the living room when she ... I mean Dad used to sleep there too, at least until he got his restraining order."

"I don't remember that. How old was I then?"

"I don't know. I guess you were five or six. Something like that."

"... ... Can't you remember anything good. A trip or something. A day when we went out somewhere, or when you did?"

"Yeah ... back then when you still hung on to Daddy's prick. A trip to the zoo ... One of the first ones it must've been. At any rate I'd really been looking forward to it. Especially to the monkeys. And then there was me standing in my fucking buggy looking down at the monkeys, and then I happened to shit myself. And you could say that wasn't popular."

"... Was it Dad who pinched you?"

"Mum it was. Yeah, you must have had a couple in your time."

"And when you got home?"

"Nothing special. I got a bit of a beating. No, the worst of it was that that was the end of the trip. Apart from that, we didn't really ... go out. We were mostly just home. Going out to play and stuff that wasn't really something we were allowed to do. That's the way it was for you too ... yeah ...

Yeah and then there was Dad. He always had such a job getting up in the mornings because of all the booze.

The other builders used to have to come and get him. But then he always had the craziest excuses. The big headache thing you know – as an excuse. Sometimes it was just so much bullshit, but sometimes it was true enough. I don't think he could really take his drink, and he couldn't let it alone either. And he just used to lie there the next day squealing like a pig, ha, ha. And then he just used to have another one. And it was always us that had to go and get his beers for him.

Either us or Mum. Yeah, and you. You never lifted a finger ... But the days when he was really in a bad way, then you had to be really quiet. Everywhere. They shut the door into the living room, and you could just creep about if it was something important like. And whisper and use sign language, you know.

So if I wasn't in school I was in the bedroom. And if Mum wasn't at work, well, then she must be in the kitchen.

Dad took down the doorbell and put it up again in the kitchen with a lead and a button into the living room. So if he wanted something, he just pressed the button and the bell rang out in the kitchen. He, he. I want one of those too."

"That's not funny, for fuck's sake. It' sick."

"Fuck that, man. It's a very smart system. And Dad he was a good sort, not a bad word to say about him."

"... You're not serious."

"Well yeah, there was a day actually where it got a bit to out of control. You were there too man. We all got called into the living room, remember? And it was me who did it ... Dad didn't want us going through his stuff, eh? And definitely not his desk. And he always knew exactly where everything lived. He was a bit of a perfectionist. Don't you remember?"

Christian shrugged his shoulders and bit his tongue.

"He asked if it was me or one of the others. And when I didn't answer, you started to fucking cry. Well, then I had to admit it, didn't I? Because otherwise he'd have taken you. You hadn't even been home. Yeah, you'd been in kindergarten, and Birgitte had been in school, or wherever. She wasn't home anyway so ... So it was fair enough.

So Dad sent you and Birgitte out again, and then called me over to him. He seemed friendly enough, smiling you know. It wasn't till I got right up close that he hit. That made the blow more powerful see. And that taught me something, really. That was a clever trick. And then I started to wail didn't I, and he comforted me on his lap.

And then just as I was quietening down again, then he fucking hit me again. That was a bit much, wasn't it. Ha, ha, ha. It's funny to look back on it though."

"... ... What about the days when we were all home? At the weekends?"

"Not much. We weren't allowed to do anything."

"I remember playing outside."

"That didn't happen very fucking often. And when it did, we had to be back again before we'd even gone out. But then there was the Kingdom Hall of course."

"The Kingdom Hall?"

"Yeah, fuck, don't you remember? That was fucking religious man. He used to come around all the time. And then we did it too, of course. Yeah, so you and I got stuffed into a pair of black trousers and a white shirt, you know, and Birgitte had a real nice dress on, you know, all ironed and everything. And then we got lined up tallest first, with you at the end, and Birgitte in the middle even though she was the eldest. It was kinda peculiar if you ask me.

And then we all tramped off to the Jehovah's Witnesses. He told Mum to have dinner ready when we came home – and where we always had to eat with our right hands of course, even though you were left-handed. But I don't remember much about any of that any more. Not apart from the discipline, they made a big number out of that. And of course you always got a couple of slaps if you couldn't get it together to eat properly. So you can't have been that small. And they always told us that God saw everything! All our 'impure thoughts,' you know. 'Satan's work.' Do you get me? Thoughts that tried to tempt you with 'worldly pleasures,' you know. Pussy, pussy, pussy, pussy.

Thomas laughed loudly before he continued:

"Dad threatened you with Satan of course. You were the youngest so he could still pull that sort of stunt on you. Said that if you didn't behave then Satan would fly up to your bedroom window and drag you down with him to hell. Uuuhhh! Can't you remember the evening when you got sent to bed alone and me and Birgitte stayed up?"

"Yeah."

"Yeah, or the time when we tried to hide you behind the door out to the bathroom, you know. The time when Dad almost throttled me with a tie. Just after that business in the living room. Where he was naked and everything. That was a bit far out, you know.

It all went totally quiet in my head. Yeah, I mean there was really a load of screaming and shouting, you know, but just then I couldn't take it.

We'd done something very, very forbidden, like he said. It was actually you who heard them first. I guess Birgitte was on her paper round. And we couldn't help ourselves, could we? So we crept out to the hall and up to the living room door which was open a crack so that we could get a peek. Do you remember?

Dad standing on the table with Mum's head covering his ... you know, his prick? We giggled of course, but we were fucking terrified. We knew what it was all about, at least I did anyway, but we'd never seen it in real life had we? Well I mean you hadn't anyway ...

And then we were caught in the act ... he must have heard us, seen us or something, I guess.

And then all hell broke loose. And then I shoved you out to the toilet. Just before he went berserk. And then it was all just like one of those silent films, you know. And Mum, stark naked, she stopped him just in time ... That was pretty heavy, as I remember it ... And then Dad locked Mum in the bedroom, and took us into the living room.

Still bullock naked and still ... he, he. Still ramrod. You know, stiff cock, hair swept back. That was not good. And then he got hold of that coat-hanger. You know, the one he'd put nails in. Do you remember that? We used to get that a lot.

I was the oldest, right, so he took me last ... really took

his time. I fucking remember, I had puke in my mouth you know. Straight up. So I had to swallow it. I didn't dare do anything else, you know. Yeah and then I just had to take what was coming to me didn't I? There wasn't really much else to do was there? But what happened, happened, what exactly it was, I don't really remember well enough any more. I was only about 9-10 years old so. But I learnt something."

"... ...?"

"I mean, I can kind of understand him. I mean Dad, you know. It's not like we were easy, is it? And then there was all that shit with Birgitte. Riing, riing. Is that the bell? Ha, ha."

Christian shook his head slowly.

"Oh come on. You can remember that. The bell that rang twice?! Don't you remember we called it the SS-sign? Sister-Signal, he he. Yeah, well then we shut up anyway, went really quiet all of us. Just sat there whilst she closed her homework book or whatever it was and got up. I remember actually from earlier, too. But then it was worse. Then she always used to jump, when the bell rang."

"Because ..."

"What?"

"Just go on."

"... Even the days when it wasn't for her. But after a while it was as if it didn't matter to her, so it can't have been that bad. She was fucking strong though. And Mum, she just sat out in the kitchen smoking like a fucking chimney – didn't make a sound. Actually I remember the flat as totally quiet, actually. With just this sort of tension in the air. You know like electricity, a sort of buzzing sound. It was just that it was so high that you almost couldn't hear it.

Especially the day when Mum had the day off work or something. She was home anyway. And we we're standing there out in the kitchen, you know, me and Mum, when Dad rang. Yeah, I guess you were in kindergarten or something ... And when Birgitte walked past on her way into the living room she just stopped suddenly and turned to Mum. She wasn't angry or anything. She just stood there, stood there for absolutely fucking ages.

And then there was Mum, her gaze all sort of broken, just got up and stood there staring stupidly out of the window. And then she just began crying. Just like that. But Birgitte's look, you know, I don't think I'll ever forget that.

And then, well it had to come I suppose, what we'd all been waiting for. Dad caught in the act, as they say. We must have had the day off school that day. I guess it was a Saturday.

Dad had hit the roof because of something or other. Yet again. Yeah, he was jealous, that was it. It wasn't the first time that had happened, I mean. I mean it wasn't the first time the police had been round. It happened a lot, but they never really did anything. But this time they couldn't really not take him with them.

Dad had kicked Mum down the stairs. You know the concrete stairs outside the flats? And her head had whacked the edge of the step, so she was lying their bleeding like anyone's business.

If only he'd not kicked her, the stupid spastic. But of course he had to keep at it, even though the cops told him to stop. So there he was hammering her like some fucking sack of potatoes. It was too much man. He couldn't treat her like that.

He'd got it into his head that Mum was up to something with the bloke from the newsagents where she worked. I mean fair enough, that's wrong. But that was it for him, last we saw of him. He never came back. But it didn't really make things much better did it, I mean.

Well, the two of us, we ended up in a children's home. I don't know why really. It must have had something to do with Mum not being able to cope, you know. Us kids just running around all the time – too much, like I said. You'd think it was the fucking stone age or something. They were a bunch of fucking arseholes, anyway and they treated us like shit. Do you remember all that stuff about having to eat what was served?"

Christian nodded without saying anything.

"I mean you really hated rice pudding. And that was what there was that day. And you threw the whole lot up onto the plate. And then those fuckers just said that you had to finish it. And you did it. Puke and all. No shit. I take my hat off to you. Respect, little brother.

But it wasn't long before we were back again. I guess we were there for six months or something. But it was a bloody hard six months I can tell you, yeah, bloody hard. For you, anyway. You were complete head fuck after that. That's what I remember. The other homes were no sweat after that place. Don't you think?"

"Well, then what?"

"Yeah, then Birgitte moved out. Half a year or so after Dad, I guess. A bit early, maybe. I don't think she was even 16 at the time. But she was ready for a bit of this and that sooo ... But she'd turned a little strange, if you ask me. Never said a word. Just went to school and went to work. Total head case. But I think anyway that I could sense something about her. Something cool. When she left, I mean. When it was time to start again, turn over a new leaf isn't that what they say? But then she snuffed it.

"Yeah ... I never really found out how that happened."

"Mum's actually really upset that you never visit her. You know that, don't you?"

"What happened to Birgitte?"

"You've turned into a little dirt grubber. Haven't you, eh?"

Christian shrugged his shoulders.

"Do you know what happened?"

"... ... Well she found this bloke see. Who she didn't really swing with anyway, or what the fuck do I know. And they had this kid together. But when she wanted out, he took the kid, right, out to the garage and did himself in and took the little one with him. You know, a hose straight from the exhaust and that was that. Actually a really good way to die, so I hear. Anyway, that was really fucked up. I mean fuck the bloke, he was just a fucking animal. But the kid man. Stupid fucker, I mean you don't fucking do that, do you? Not with a kid, eh?! Not with a bloody kid. Anyway, I think it was all a bit too much for her. And they found her with her wrists cut or some such. I think there were some pills involved too. Something like that. Anyway, she was definitely finito. And I guess we're actually pretty alike in that respect. I mean, there's no way I'd do myself in, but when there are kids involved I get angry. I bloody do. Nobody touches my kids. You get me. So I guess I can understand that she went a bit cold. What a fucking fag. If he'd had enough he could just fuck off, couldn't he? He didn't have to take the kid. Fucking faggot ..."

"Then what?"

"What?"

"Well, you know, everything, I mean?"

"Yeah, that was it really. You ended up in boarding school or something, and I just stayed home and went to school until I took off and went to sea. And Mum she moved in with the boyfriend, and took revenge for all the money you know."

"You went to boarding school too didn't you?"

"Yeah sure but just for a year. I never went to school much. I couldn't really see the point. The others were such a bunch of pricks, and they couldn't teach me anything anyway. It all went okay at the start. But then I got called up to the headmaster's office, you know, for a chat, with Mum. It wasn't good enough, I never came to school, blah, blah, blah. And they'd given me chances, so now there weren't going to be any more. And there was this rumour that it was me who'd been nicking a lot of stuff here and there. That was all lies of course. Well not, really, obviously, but I wasn't letting on was I, he, he. So they kicked me out. I was supposed to go to boarding school like you, but that only lasted a year. Yeah, you had it worse. In and out, back and forth, home and school. I can't remember you being home at all. Not much anyway."

"I didn't come back till after tenth grade."

"Oh yeah, that's right. By then I was well on my way."

"What was that stuff about the police? I remember Mum flipping out because you got arrested or something."

"Oh, yeah. That was actually just before boarding school."

"What had you done?"

"Jack shit, man. It was just some crap they pinned on me because I was in the area when it happened.
But I didn't make a fuss. What was there to say? They were going to send me away anyway. Without me doing anything. But it was okay. They couldn't get to me."

"Yeah, okay, but what had you done?"

"Fuck all I said! Are you fucking deaf or what?!"

"... ..."

"It was something about some bitch that said that I was supposed to have stood jerking off at her for weeks or something. And there wasn't anything in it okay?!"

"Okay."

"Fuck you, man."

"What is it? I said okay, didn't I?"

"They said something like that I'd stood in her garden. And because I happened to be there when the cops showed up they did me for it. They had to pick up someone or other didn't they? And when I couldn't explain how come I was there. Well ... that was that."

"So then it was boarding school?"

"... One year, then I came back again. Yeah, they said I was out of control. Wasn't my fucking fault though. I had to smash some guy in the face already on the first day to defend myself like. It wasn't my kind of place. He just came up to me and started hitting me. What the fuck, I mean. Yeah, so I had to defend myself, like. Nothing wrong with that. And it was better than staying home. Alone. But I guess you had your fair share of that. She didn't come home when I took off did she? ... ... I guess I was a bit of a handful. Stole fags and stuff from the supermarkets, but anyway. It could have been a lot worse. And by then, well I'd had enough. The others said I'd done something or other to some girl, and I just wasn't having it. So I took off.

I did my school work and all that. They let me change room so I could live on my own."

"What was it they said you did. You were saying?"

"Fuck all. Really. It was actually fuck all. We'd had this party see, on a Friday or a Saturday, and one of the girls got really drunk, stupid mare and had to go to bed. And there was me needed a slash, but I couldn't find the toilet, and of course I end up in this cow's room. One of the other guys had seen me go in, and he called the others. And then they pulled me out and there was a bit of a set to. That was all. Faggots. If they'd tried that again, I'd have finished them, I can tell you. All of 'em."

"So nothing happened to the girl, I mean?"

"Not a fucking thing. Of course she said I'd tried to get into bed with her."

"Why'd she say that?"

"I don't fucking know. Because she was a stupid mare. I'd been sitting chatting with her all evening, you know.

After that I just kept myself to myself. And the next year it was back to Mum, not that she was ever there, but ..."

"And then you went on the ships ..."

"Yeah, several times. I think I did that for five maybe six years. It was okay. Container ships. I saw loads of places. Plenty of pussy. It was cool."

"But?"

"But what? Yeah, well then I had to give that up.

Nearest port you know. No messing about there. They said I'd broken the customs seal on something or other. Why the fuck would I want to do that? And there was something or other about some of the others being a bit short or something. Yeah, they even put it in my discharge book. So I had to leave the ship in Miami. Not a bad thing really, if only I'd had a little more money. But what the hell. I saw the place. Then it was back to Denmark. And I couldn't really get a berth anywhere, sooo. So I answered this ad in the paper. Cleaning, you know. I mean you've got to do something haven't you. And no experience needed, they'd help you learn it and all that.

It was a pretty big company actually. With company cars and lots of people there, you know. And it was actually the boss himself showed me the ropes. Well, the wife, you know. A real chick, I mean. A real chick. I only saw the bloke when we had to drive on to the next job.

But of course then it all started to fuck up again. It all started with this bulb that wanted changing. The wife had this little ladder, and she asked me to change a bulb on the third floor. I clambered up of course, and began to twist the old bulb out, you know, whilst she stood there and made sure that I didn't fall down, as she said. He, he. And it was then that she suddenly put her hand on my cock. Ha!

That made me fucking nervous, of course. I mean what about her old man and all that, eh? But she took things very calm, very easy.

Then we drove on to the next place. With the husband doing the driving, and me sitting on the back seat together with the wife. And she unzips me trousers, and puts me cock in her gob. It was pretty far out.

A couple of days later she asked if I wanted to go home with her. The husband out, evidently. Away on business or some such.

But when we were lying there in the bed, I heard this noise from the lobby. And of course I asked what it was. I didn't want to get a nasty surprise from the husband now, did I? But this bird, she was completely unflustered, and then well, that could just as well be that, couldn't it?

But when the bloke suddenly stood there bullock naked like in the doorway, well then I thought it was all getting a bit much. And I was pretty close to beating the crap out of both of them I don't mind saying, especially him.

Anyway, I got myself a room in the suburbs somewhere. It was okay.

And I still worked, you know, for that cleaning company. I was with them for years like. They asked me, you know, whether I wanted to come with them on holiday. That was actually pretty far out. Up to their snobby summer house up north somewhere. They were good people, so that was fine by me.

And it was a really nice house too. Enormous and with a sea view an' everything.

And loads of rooms – with bunk beds. And I got one of those all to myself. With a toilet and a shower, the works. And the wife, well she came in to me every night. And sometimes in the garden, or on the beach. I forgot about the husband completely. Most of the time he just stood there watching anyway. And if that was how he got his kicks well, I didn't mind. They were good times. Sunshine, trips on the beach and summer evenings and cold beer and a barbecue – the works. It was all pretty cool.

And then there was this thing with Tina. She was one of the tarts from work, we used to say hello, you know how it is. But I'd never really thought about her. She was about the same age as me. About twenty-four I'd say. A skinny little thing, you know. Thin with this dead sort of hair. Green eyes, small tits. Not my sort of piece. But quite all right really, of course.

Of course it was the wife and the husband who'd arranged it all. You could feel it straight away. I mean there were no games when Tina was there. That was okay, because we got a bit more time for each other, you know. I mean Tina and me.

And the first night we did it properly, you know. After a load of booze and food and all that. I tell you she was good. I can tell you. Straight to it. No fucking around as you might say. He, he. It was cool, she was very inventive. And the husband and wife, well they'd just left us to it, left us in peace, you know.

Well, d'you know what happened then? Well, we

started going out, for real. I mean, we was still colleagues for a while and all that. Anyway, so I took my driving license, and started looking for something else to do. You know, a job that was a bit better, maybe. Not that the one I hadn't wasn't fine. It was a good job, but just washing stairs all the time, you get to a point where you've had enough of it. Yeah and Tina was pregnant so we had to get married. In the town hall. That was okay. No nonsense there, you know, just in and out, and that was it.

So it ended up with her as a housewife in the new flat we got from the council. They have loads of empty flats round about so it would seem. Yeah, and Arnold was on his way."

"Yeah?"

"I called him after Schwarzenegger, you know. A really good kid if you ask me. Yeah, everything looked really cushtie. But Tina and the kid, you know. Yeah, he's a fucking smart little one. If only I hadn't had to go through all this piss. It's not because I regret what I did or anything ..."

"Weren't you in for drugs at one point? ..."

"Fuck, man! Not again. Look, I can't take much more of this shit. What I've done had absolutely fuck all to do with that, okay?! When the fuck are you going to understand that?! Drugs are for niggers. *Towel heads* think it makes them white. It's just something the cops made up for some fucking stupid twisted reason of their own."

"What was it then, if it wasn't drugs?"

"Vitamin pills, man. Call them vitamin pills for sportsmen. And in any case, I never did what I was sent down for."

"But they put you away, right?"

"Six months, man. And so what? And I got through most of it whilst I was in protective custody."

"And you don't think it's got anything to do with what now ... I mean all that stuff with Dad?"

"Not a fucking thing mate. Those are two completely different things."

Thomas reached out and grabbed Christian's watch."

"Fuck. The hour's up. I'm going to have to go up now. Look, drop by Tina okay and take something with you next time, okay?!"

"Thomas, I ..."

"Look, I'll get you the address, have you got something to write with? Ask her why the fuck she never comes to see me any more. They only let me out every once in a while. And it's my kid, for fuck's sake! And remember to take something with you next time, okay?!"

"What?"

"What? What?! 'Ave you got a fucking screw loose? Something. Whatever. Some stuff you can bring in under your shirt that we can sort out here. Yeah, some coke or something. You'll think of something. I just can't take it up with me. They check you everywhere, head and arse. And I mean arse."

# 10

He'd not read them. Had just left them there unread. Although, of course he knew what to expect. Pretty much. Christian flicked through the folder Tina had given him. Left the first couple which were all about break-ins and stopped at a couple of the next ones.

**Student attacked at cemetery square**

A 21-year-old female student contacted the police to report an attack which took place in the early hours of yesterday morning.

The 21-year-old, who was on her way to university, had taken her usual route by bicycle across the cemetery when a boy of between 14 and 16 years of age jumped out and took hold of her. When the young woman resisted, the assailant fled, and the woman escaped with minor abrasions.

Police sources say that an alarming pattern is emerging, and that this is the third such attack within a month. "This would suggest that it's the same individual who's behind these attacks. But at this stage it's far to early to draw any firm conclusions," said police spokesman Henning Larsen. Currently the police have no leads and would be grateful for any help they can receive from the general public.

The assailant is described as Danish, 14 to 16 years old, about 180 cm tall, of normal build, with greasy blonde hair and blue eyes. The boy was wearing a grey jumper, jeans and trainers. Any witnesses to this attack or previous assaults are asked to contact the police on the following number: 44 44 14 48.

(al)

**Woman raped on her way home from work**

In the early hours of yesterday morning a 46-year-old woman was attacked and raped by an unknown assailant.

The woman, who was found lying unconscious on the edge of a woodland path by a passing jogger, told police that she had crawled out to the path in an attempt to escape, but that she then fell unconscious.

The 46-year-old was on her way home from work on her bicycle, when she was suddenly attacked by a man with a moped who had stopped and appeared to be repairing it on the edge of the forest path. Initially the man pulled a bag over the woman's head and she was then pulled away from the path and threatened with a sharp object, in all likelihood a knife. When the woman seemingly was not quick enough in obeying her assailant, she was kicked to the point of unconsciousness.

The woman is still hospitalised with concussion and has suffered several broken ribs.

Police sources say that the rapist was unusually violent and ask any potential witnesses to come forth. The victim was only able to provide a vague description of her assailant, however he is described as being between 20 and 30 years of age, and was wearing a crash helmet and a dark blue jacket.

Police have called in extra resources in their attempt to bring the assailant to justice and can be contacted on the following number: 44 44 14 48.

(al)


Christian flipped through the pages of the folder to the next major story. A spectacular two-page tabloid article from one of the nationals.

Before reading the article proper he sat for a long time and just concentrated on the individual words in the article's heading. Words which, to most people, would seem innocent and insignificant. It was only in context that it really made sense.

Whereas the article had been florid and emotional, the folder's final page was brief and to the point. A formal document. An indictment.


"And cut!"

## II

There was an obelisk on the square. With pictures and inscriptions on all four sides. At the edge of the square there was a bench. And along one side of the square and positioned somewhat unfortunately relative to everything else was a rectangular granite tub with flowers in it.

Christian stopped opposite the obelisk. Studied the new classicist building on the other side of the square and wondered at the somewhat misplaced tower. Stepped a couple of meters back and took everything in.

The exterior of the building was dominated by six Doric columns which supported the portico. On the left hand side was a statue of David, whilst Moses was to the right.

The relief frieze immediately above the door was partially concealed behind the columns, and was not as prominent as perhaps it should have been. Apart from that the building was just big. It dominated the square.

Christian mounted the low steps and continued through the open wooden doors. Stood momentarily considering his reflection in the enormous glass partition, but followed a woman with a couple of medium-sized kids into the interior of the building.

Once inside, he paused for a while surprised and uncertain of his next move. Taken aback by the noise. He'd expected a bit more reverence. Quiet. There were several groups of school children on trips, and they hadn't the concentration to just sit and listen to what was told them. Some of them were running round taking pictures with their mobile phones, others just played in-between the benches. Christian suddenly felt the need to visit the toilet.

He looked around and instinctively chose to turn left. Hoped that the disturbances would disappear if he just gave them time. Several doors with signs for all sorts of other things, but he was driven onwards by a sound. A snore which turned out to emanate from a sleeping alchy on a bench. Right outside the toilet he'd been hoping to use. The door was locked. There was a piece of paper on it which said that the toilet was only available during services. Probably not the best time to visit the loo, thought Christian. In any case, he no longer felt the need.

Christian wandered back and stood for a while just considering the unwonted space. A large nave and a throned Jesus standing with open arms above the alter. Further back there was a marble angel with a crown of flowers in her hair. She was holding a giant mussel in her arms. The font, of course.

Christian let his gaze wander around. Took a step back and his attention was drawn to four identical circular light fittings in the ceiling, each with 16 drab spotlights that cast a weak light over the space. Next he saw a sculpture, a sort of globe on which there several small lit candles. Discretely arranged in the far-most corner of the nave. He turned and his gaze fell on a statue to his left. He approached it. Strangely attracted by the statue's thoughtful expression. He wondered at the over-sized angle iron in the statue's lap. Christian gaze fell to the plaque at the bottom, but was disappointed not to find any explanation of what the tool symbolised.

His errand was still clear, if unarticulated. His feelings were clear. And yet he had difficulty finding the necessary calm. Yet surprisingly patient, both with himself and with the noisy crowds. He sat and waited on one of the many benches about half way into the church. All of which were equipped with red plastic cushions, small speakers in the back of the next row of seats and small lamps at the end. Further forward the benches were different. Christian counted. The first six rows on each side of the aisle were double ones. Like miniature open railway carriages. It seemed as if sitting with your back to the alter during a service was actually encouraged, thought Christian.

A couple of tourists and their young daughter walked past, and move quickly to one side when a couple of boys came walking past with a couple of crates of soft drinks. Up to the children's choir who had just finished practising. The tourists returned to their original course, whilst the daughter moved ahead of them and, finally, ran off in another direction. Americans evidently. The parents were speaking English with American accents.

Christian sat waiting still and spent his time studying the decorations. Because now he had time. All the time he needed. He counted the twelve statues, six on each side, all standing on grey, worn, marble plinths and concluded that they must be the 12 apostles. He tried to remember their names, but interrupted himself by reading an inscription on the pulpit. He could only make out the last of it though. It was a reference to the Bible: 'Luke XI, 28'.

Christian turned his attention to the figure of Jesus. Framed by a couple of marble columns, it reminded him of a mausoleum as much as anything else. There were two large candles on the actual alter. Neither of them were lit. And at the extremities on both sides, two strangely misplaced street lamps stood. Christian found it hard to place them in relation to the rest of the things in the church, but didn't find them shameful. Peculiar was probably a better word. Just like so many other things. It made no sense having them there.

The groups of school children were on their way out again, and there didn't seem to be any others on their way in. Christian sensed that someone was looking at him and turned to see the tourists' little daughter who just stood there looking at him in silence. Christian nodded at her in a friendly way and smiled at her brown eyes. Gently. The girl didn't react, just stood there.

"Caridad, what are you doing?"

The mother came and took her hand.

"Sorry 'bout that."

"It's all right," answered Christian smiling. "No problem. How old is she?"

"Seven," answered the mother smiling as she made her way towards the waiting father.

Christian nodded and followed them with his eyes. Next, at the exit, the girl turned around. This time she lifted her hand and waved. "Bye."

Christian waved back at her, and knew now that the church was empty.

He got up. Moved deliberately towards the alter and read the words above the throned figure. '*This is my son in whom I am well pleased.*'

He noticed the discrete wound in the figure's side, doubted and was suddenly unsure of his own feelings. He let the pictures into his mind and knelt down as if it was the most natural thing in the world. He found a slight tremor leaving his body and had already seen the first blow. The blow that was so violent that it had broken his father's cheek bone. The blow that had been the first of so many. And suddenly he could hear his father's shouts, whilst Thomas was deadly quiet.

Quiet and ferocious, systematically working his way further and further up. More and more bloodily, with the shouts gradually replaced by slushy noises. Dumb, slushy noises from the blows that just kept on raining down. Again, and again, and again, whilst the face, especially the face, was transformed into meat. All human features, all human contours and all human senses smashed and gone for ever.

No crying. Only the acceptance. The insight. The understanding. For them both. Mostly.

Outside someone had put a sign up. A big sign but one he hadn't previously noticed. Christian unzipped his jacket as he savoured some of the laconic sentences. '*A God's house*' – '*a place of worship.*'
He drew breath heavily and repeatedly and was overwhelmed by a sensation that something was missing. As if there was something he had forgotten. Or ... something he had suddenly lost. He put his head on one side and listened. All he could hear was ... silence. The perpetual grinding and urgent dialogue with himself about what he should and shouldn't do had suddenly stopped. As if it had never existed. The thing which previously had so dominated his personality was now gone.
The feeling was greater than simple relief at having shaken it off. Greater than simply having solved a given problem. It was happier. Deeper. Like a realisation

and something obvious at one and the same time. Like something natural, that after an unnatural absence had suddenly fallen into place again.

A bubbling and clucking laughter unfolded in Christian's stomach and spread throughout his chest. And Christian had to laugh. Laugh as he had never laughed before. Without vanity, without reserve. Just a pure and crystal clear laughter, that the people who happened to be passing took to themselves. Afterwards the air seemed extra pure.

He looked up and down the street and entered the throng, and wondered whether to just call Natasha. Instead he hailed a taxi and seconds later he was on his way to the place where her parents lived. It was a long way, but he knew the route so it felt shorter. Now.


The first assistant director repeats the director's 'cut' over the walkie-talkie, so everyone knows that they're no longer recording. Two short buzzers succeed the killing of the flashing 'red-eye,' indicating to people outside the sound stage that they'd stopped shooting.

"Let's have a look, shall we."

The actors move over to the monitor to watch while everything is wound back to the start of the take. Everyone's happy, and the serious, almost depressed atmosphere, has evaporated like morning dew.

"Okay, camera's moving. To a medium shot seen from the opposite side."

The assistant director spreads his fingers to indicate where the camera is to be positioned.

"We're now pointing in that direction. So everything that's not in the picture needs to be moved. Come on, let's get moving, people. We haven't got all day. Not any more."

A natural change in focus and concentration that results in a just as rapid prop change.

The property master and the props assistants run back and forth. Furniture gets moved around. Things, pictures, knick-knacks.

Some lamps are turned off, others get turned on. The stills photographer creeps around taking pictures. The sound mixer pushes his little cart with all his bits and bobs on it into a more convenient corner. The art director and a couple of her assistants are moving the wall so there's more room for the camera.

The cinematographer tells the assistant director that he's going out to get himself a cup of coffee, but is stopped by the producer and the production manager who come in carrying a long cake with sparklers and candles.

Everyone crowds round the director and begins singing the familiar birthday song.

"... Congratulations!!!"

"How old are you going to be? Forty-seven?"

They all laugh.

"Almost. Thirty-four ... thanks," he says. "Thanks really."